Wrong Brother, Right Match

an Anyone but You novel

Wrong Brother, Right Match

an Anyone but You novel

JENNIFER SHIRK

Entangled Publishing, LLC
2614 South Timberline Road
Suite 109
Fort Collins, CO 80525
Visit our website at www.entangledpublishing.com.

Bliss is an imprint of Entangled Publishing, LLC. For more information on our titles, visit http://www.entangledpublishing.com/category/bliss

Edited by Stacy Abrams
Cover design by Melody Pond
Cover art from iStock

Manufactured in the United States of America

First Edition December 2016

Bliss

For my intelligent, funny, beautiful teenaged daughter, who actually admitted on Instagram that I was cool. I'm forever saving that post!

Chapter One

Kennedy Pepperdine's life could not be more perfect.

Well, technically it *could* be, she supposed. That half-baked rival matchmaking firm that opened up six months ago could go belly-up, and *then* her life really would be set. But for right now, her business, Match Made Easy, was holding its own, she'd just delivered a successful presentation on her new matchmaking software, and—best of all—she was in love.

Perfect.

Thoughts drifting to her perfect boyfriend, Kennedy pulled out her cell phone as she made her way through the Chairman's Lounge of the Bellagio hotel. Since arriving in Vegas for the Creative Technology Developer Conference four days ago, she and Justin had only had time to exchange voicemail messages. Justin worked at the Briarwood Investments firm in Boston, and he had been adamant about it being the worst possible time to leave and that his workload simply would not allow it.

Although disappointed, she couldn't fault him for wanting to get ahead in his firm. She felt the same way about her own business. They were both workaholics, they both wanted 2.5 kids and a dog, and they shared the same *Game of Thrones* TV-watching obsession—which was why they were so perfect for each other.

Her matchmaking software was obviously a success.

She'd tested it on herself early in its initial phase, which was how she met Justin in the first place. It was just the break she needed for her company. The numbers proved Match Made Easy was taking a hit from the competition, so she'd needed to come up with something fast before her business was in real danger. However, now she needed to get back to her hotel room. Her feet throbbed, and her mouth was dry from speaking. All she wanted to do was share her day with Justin and take a long, hot bath. But as soon as she tapped his name on her cell phone, it rang once and went right to voicemail. Again.

She gritted her teeth. At this rate, she considered herself going steady with that stupid automated message.

"Hi, sweetie, it's me—Kennedy. *Again*." She winced at herself for adding the "again" part. She never wanted to be one of those petulant girlfriend types. "Um, I just finished my presentation and everything went great. Just wanted you to know my flight leaves early tomorrow morning. Can't wait to see you." *And finally speak to you.* "Hope everything is good. Miss you." She clicked her phone off and tossed it in her purse.

Not a big deal, she reminded herself for the sixth time this weekend. Lots of executive couples went days—*weeks*, even—without speaking to each other. A part of today's urban culture. It had absolutely nothing to do with him not missing her. Except…

Well…

Wouldn't he have tried to call her in the middle of the night? Wouldn't he have needed to hear her voice at least once during her trip? Maybe even when he first woke up in the morning before he got out of bed and started his day?

No. No way. She refused to let any more doubt cloud her opinion of him or their relationship. He was handsome and driven and everything she was looking for in a man. So what if he couldn't find the time to call her?

She picked up her pace to the elevator and counted herself lucky—dang lucky—for even finding such a focused, hardworking boyfriend. The man was a complete prince and always there for her when she truly needed him.

She glanced around the spacious entryway. The elevators were off to the left. She hated elevators—actually, she hated small spaces in general. Much like airplanes, they were a necessary evil in life, so she dashed in that direction. She was already contemplating her exact room service order when she saw the up elevator doors open, but then they almost immediately began to close again.

Oh, no! "Hold the elevator, please!" She pressed her briefcase to her chest as her heels pounded the marble flooring as fast as her tippy toes would allow.

Just when she thought she'd missed her chance and would be stuck waiting, a large hand shot out, keeping the doors from closing. *Thank goodness.* The elevators were beyond slow because of the huge conference crowd. Huffing and puffing—she really should visit her cousin's gym more—she stumbled into the elevator with dizzying relief.

She caught her breath and finally looked up into the eyes of her saving grace, only to have her lungs deflate all over again. *Oh, dear heaven above.* She actually melted a little, grateful the wall of the elevator kept her somewhat upright. Elevator Guy was ridiculously gorgeous. So gorgeous that despite the jeans, sensible blue collared shirt, and blazer ensemble he was sporting, she still had to wonder if he was a headliner at the Chippendales show next door. He had sandy brown hair that was in need of a good trim and just a teensy bit of facial hair that was somewhere between a five o'clock shadow and a short beard. All that combined with the intensely serious expression on his face made him seem just a little bit dangerous. But dangerous in a good way.

A *very* good way.

That is, if she were into handsome, dangerous men and wasn't already in a fantastic relationship with a handsome man of her own.

The hunk suddenly shifted away and sent her a hesitant smile. That's when she realized she was gawking. Great, he didn't even know her, and she was already labeled a stalker. She could only hope drool wasn't glistening off her chin.

She cleared her throat and tried to rectify her first impression. "Um, thanks for holding the elevator."

"My pleasure," he said, his deep voice vibrating through her chest. "What floor?"

"Floor? Why do you want to know my floor?"

He simply raised a brown eyebrow.

Oh. Right. He was going to press the button for her. Duh. Heat rushed to her cheeks. "Twenty-four, please." *Snap out of it, Kennedy.*

He pressed her floor number for her and—just out of curiosity, mind you—she noticed he was going to one floor above hers. Or most likely to his girlfriend's floor. A giant bottle of champagne was secured under his arm and two champagne flutes dangled from his left hand. He was probably heading up there now to surprise her.

Lucky girl.

She would have given anything to have Justin surprise her like that. He rarely did anything spontaneous. She was about to berate herself for thinking such negative thoughts when the lights flickered a few times then went out completely.

The elevator came to an abrupt stop, and she braced her

hand on the wall to keep from losing her balance.

"Oh my gosh, what's happening?" she choked out. Her pulse skyrocketed. Immediate thoughts went to the chance there was a broken elevator cable or a possible fire. Or a terrorist plot! Unfortunately, being an avid movie watcher, she knew a little too well all the countless tragedies associated with elevators.

Her briefcase fell to the floor with a thud, and she held her head in both hands, trying to take deep, slow breaths. The air already seemed thin. Ohmygosh, she was going to die. She was going to suffocate if she didn't drop to her death first. She never had a chance to say good-bye to her family, her friends. To Justin. She had to escape.

Hands poised and ready to begin clawing her way out, she suddenly noticed Elevator Guy turn on the flashlight app on his cell phone and press the emergency button. Using the light to guide him, he flipped a small metal latch beneath the floor buttons and pulled out a hidden phone, as if getting stuck in an elevator was an everyday occurrence for him.

Oh, no. Maybe he's *the terrorist!* She felt even woozier.

"Hello," he said into the receiver. He listened for a few seconds then began pressing each floor button in a slow, methodical sequence. "No, none of the buttons are working, and yes, everyone here is fine." With a raised eyebrow, he cast a wary side glance her way. "Relatively fine."

Hey! Now, what is that *supposed to mean?*

She planted her fists on her hips and bore a hole right through the side of his head with her glare. This guy wasn't nearly as handsome as she'd originally thought. Not at all. He was only *marginally* handsome at best.

"Okay, we'll sit tight, then," he said into the phone. "Thanks for your help." He hung up and turned to her. "The good news is they know that we're here and that the elevator is stuck."

Her shoulders wilted. "What's the bad news, then?"

"We might be here awhile until they figure out what the glitch is."

She blinked. "Glitch? This is a multimillion-dollar, five-hundred-foot hotel. We are stuck here with no food, water, or bathroom for who knows how long, and they're calling that a *glitch*?"

"Apparently so." Elevator Guy sank down on the floor, making himself comfortable.

This is so not happening. No, no, no. She shook her head. This would not do. She was not going to just sit here and wait as he used up all her oxygen. The walls felt like they were closing in like a trash compactor. She wiped her perspiring forehead. Surely *somebody* could pull some strings and get things moving quicker. She whipped out her cell phone and tried to call Justin again. He would know what to do. He was smart and reliable and—unlike her companion here—*compassionate.*

She held the phone to her ear, tapping her toe as she waited. *Pick up the phone this time. Pick up the phone.* His voicemail message—the one she could recite by heart—began to play. She swore under her breath.

"No luck?"

Startled by his question, she frowned down at Elevator Hunk. She'd almost forgotten he was there. He sat with his legs straight out, ankles crossed. His eyes were closed. He wasn't aggravated at all that he was stuck in this hot metal death trap. In fact, it seemed as if he was actually enjoying the peace and quiet. "No," she grumbled. "No luck."

He opened his eyes and patted the space beside him. "Why don't you sit? Standing isn't going to make the doors open any sooner. And besides, you're making me anxious."

She wanted to laugh. The man looked anything but tense. She, on the other hand, was a tightly wound mess. She was already having trouble catching her breath. *Stress-induced asthma*. That's what her doctor had labeled it the first time she experienced it. Probably just a fancy diagnosis that meant: does not deal well with unexpected problems. He advised her to get enough sleep (she was working on that), do yoga regularly (totally would do once she found the time and the flexibility), and carry a paper bag with her at all times (done). Since a nap and downward-facing dog were obviously not going to happen, she pulled out a folded brown bag from her purse and began to slowly inhale and exhale into it.

The man looked up in horror. "What are you doing?"

"What does it look like I'm doing? Chest muscles tighten, caused by"—she breathed a few more times into the bag— "high stress and anxiety. I'm claustrophobic."

He squinted as if weighing her words. "You're *claustrophobic*?"

"Yes," she mumbled into the bag. "I need to get out." It was a control thing. Her mind knew that. It really did—even if her body and lungs did not.

"Okay, okay, relax," he told her, holding up splayed hands.

Ha! Easy for him to say. Sitting there like a cabana boy as if all he needed in the world was a pair of Oakleys and some sun-tanning oil. She took deeper breaths in and out. "I can't relax." The bag collapsed in. "I want out." The bag expanded out again.

He sighed, and this time his voice gentled. "Look, I want out, too, but we have to be patient. Just know that we *will* get out, so there's nothing to panic about." His gaze captured hers, direct and unwavering. "I promise you."

She paused. Looked at him closely. "You promise?" she said into the bag.

"I do."

"Okay." She nodded, and her shoulders relaxed just a smidgeon. There was something about the confidence in his

"I do" that had her believing him, and it soothed her fraying nerves.

He held up the magnum of champagne he'd had under his arm from before and waved it in front of her. "I'm thinking you could use a drink."

"Great, that's all I need when there's no bathroom around."

The man pinched the bridge of his nose and sighed. "Okay, scratch that. Now I'm thinking *I* could use a drink." Shaking his head, he began removing the foiled top.

"Please don't take an eye out." She stepped back. "Or rather, *my* eye out."

He shot her a devilish grin. "Don't worry. I've handled my share of champagne bottles. The trick is in the number six."

"The number six?" Curious and a little bit thirsty, she sank down on the floor beside him.

"Yep. Six half-turns counter-clockwise of the wired cage here—also called a muselet in case you were wondering."

"I wasn't." She smiled at him.

"Right. Well, anyway, you ease the cork out with the left hand while rotating the bottle with the right. And then..." Looking satisfied with himself, he presented the cork to her like a regular Lance Burton Master Magician wannabe. "Unlike TV, the true goal of opening champagne is to barely make a sound or spill a drop."

She pushed up her glasses and cocked her head. "Huh. You seem to know a lot about champagne. Are you a waiter or something?"

"Or something." He slowly poured the fizzing wine in each of the flutes he had with him then handed her one. "My family owns a winery."

He held out his glass, and they clinked. She tentatively took a sip and found it delicious. Elevator Guy definitely knew his wines.

"Thanks," she said. "I guess I did need this. I feel sort of bad, though. You obviously had other plans for this bottle."

He checked his watch and shrugged. "I'm sure she's given up on me by now and found new plans of her own."

"Oh. Sorry again."

"Not your fault the elevator got stuck. Besides, this bottle was a freebie. Got it at the Wine and Spirits Expo going on at the Paris across the street. This particular vendor, she loves me."

Kennedy didn't have a hard time believing that. The man looked like the type to be pretty popular with the ladies without even trying.

They both drained their glasses fairly quickly. "Might as well put this to good use," he said, picking up the bottle and topping them both off. "And I hate to even point this out, but you already stopped needing that thing." He motioned to her lap.

She looked down at the paper bag and brightened. Hey, he was right. She had forgotten all about being trapped hundreds of feet in the air...by a few measly cable ropes... with very little air...

She gulped down the rest of her champagne and held out her glass again. "Better keep it coming."

He hesitated, looking slightly amused at her insistence. "Did you have anything to eat? You should slow down if you haven't."

"Oh, *now* I get the concern. Do you want the paper bag to come out again or not?"

He laughed. "Definitely not." He poured her a fresh glass then picked up his own and held it for a toast. "Here's to coming out exactly how we came in."

"Um...straightforward if not a bit crude."

"Are you describing me or the wine?" He grinned.

She smothered a smile, clinking her glass with his, and

drank. Perhaps she'd misjudged Elevator Guy earlier. He seemed sensitive to her plight. He'd also managed to divert her attention from the situation and even make her feel more relaxed. Plus, he wasn't so hard to look at, either.

She stuck out her hand, ready to extend the olive branch. After all, she might as well make the best of it. "My name's Kennedy."

"As in the president?"

"As in my mother's *favorite* president."

"Good choice, because you don't strike me as a Van Buren."

She laughed. "That's a relief."

He grinned back and took her hand in his. "My mother wasn't as political or original. So you can just call me Matt. A pleasure to be trapped with you, Kennedy."

• • •

Matt Ellis had his initial reservations about the pretty redhead with anxiety the size of Texas, but now that she'd loosened up and stopped hyperventilating into that lunch bag of hers, she was actually quick-witted and sweet. Plus, with those funky little glasses, she had a whole sexy librarian thing going that he kind of liked, too.

"So, explain to me again what you do?" he asked, still not sure he'd heard her right the first two times.

Kennedy hiccupped then took a sip of her champagne. "I can't remember. What did I already tell you?"

"That you own a matchmaking company in Boston, which happens to be where my brother lives."

"Bingo!" She poked her finger in his chest. "How did you know that?"

"How did I know where my brother lives?"

She laughed. "No. What I do for a living."

"I'm a mind reader." He smirked. The woman was definitely feeling the effects of the alcohol. Not that he was complaining. That reserved wall had finally come down, and she appeared to be pleasantly buzzed. She nudged closer to him—so close he caught the sweet smell of her perfume. Sweet like her smile. And soft. Through her purple-framed glasses, he saw that she had soft blue eyes, too.

He cleared his throat and looked away. "Is that all?"

Her back drew upright as if he'd slapped her in the face. "What do you mean, is that all? I have a staff of twenty now, not including the array of male and female escorts I also have on hand for corporate events or weddings. In fact, we need to expand our offices and—"

He held up his hands in surrender and laughed. "Okay, okay. Easy. I didn't mean is that all your company is. I just thought you would want to tell me a little more about it."

"Oh." She looked down, her cheeks coloring. "Sorry. I'm very proud of my business. And it's just that when you're a woman CEO, you constantly find yourself on the defensive."

Smart, pretty, and a feisty entrepreneur. This woman had it all.

Suddenly, muffled classical music started playing. Kennedy grabbed her purse and pulled out her phone. "Oh, thank goodness," she cried. She glanced at the face on the screen then she smiled at him. "It's my boyfriend."

Boyfriend?

Matt swallowed the shot of disappointment he'd just been handed with the grace of a king and politely smiled back. Apparently, she really did have it all, including a friggin' boyfriend. Any chance of the two of them getting out of here and making it back to his hotel room were null and void.

"Finally!" she breathed into the phone. "Honey, you will never believe— Oh." She paused, her mouth dangling open like a bass as she listened to the other end of the line. "Yes, fine. Thanks for telling me, Fred. No, no, don't worry about it. It wasn't important anyway. Yes, you, too. 'Bye."

Without another word, she tossed her phone next to her and raised a hand to her forehead. Uh-oh. Whatever news Fred-the-boyfriend just delivered couldn't have been good.

He sidled closer, immediately wanting to comfort her. But they'd only known each other a few hours. Didn't even know each other's full names. The last thing she needed was a stranger touching her.

The silence began to hurt his ears. He finally cleared his throat, keeping his tone light. "Everything all right?"

She didn't move for a few seconds. When she finally looked up, his stomach dropped when he saw tears glistening in her eyes. "Yes, fine," she croaked.

Oh, no. Not tears. Please. He was begging God and the mother of all elevator jams that tears would not begin to fall. That was the one thing in life he could not handle well. Emotional women were his Kryptonite. It was hard enough having to take care of his mother and young sister.

"Good, then," he said with a firm nod. "Good." He needed another drink. He automatically went for the champagne bottle, but it was empty. Dammit.

She hiccupped. "He really is a great boyfriend," she explained, wringing her hands.

"Who, Fred?"

"Huh? Oh, no, not Fred. Fred is his personal assistant. He called to tell me that they were up late working on a portfolio for a very important client—a yacht builder—and that's why my boyfriend hasn't called me all weekend."

"Sounds a bit shady to me."

Her eyes widened. "Oh, no, he would never cheat on me. He's not the type. If he wanted out of the relationship, he would just be upfront."

"Really? How can you be so sure?"

"It's part of the information I acquire through my relationship software."

He stared at her for several long beats. "Relationship *software*?"

"Yes," she said, nodding so hard, her glasses slipped down her nose. "That's the whole reason I'm here in the first place. To present my software to potential investors and colleagues at the Creative Technology Conference. I tested it on myself. It's quite accurate."

"I see."

Her eyes narrowed. "No, you don't. Men only say 'I see' when they clearly do not see."

He sighed. "Fine. You got me there. But I'll tell you exactly what I *do* see. I see a bright, sensitive woman whose feelings are hurt because her boyfriend—even though overworked — still did not make the least bit of effort to show her that he cared or was thinking about her for the three—"

"Four."

"*Four?* Four days she's been away."

Kennedy grew silent again. She began chewing her bottom lip. His eyes automatically dropped to her mouth, and for the forty-eighth time since being trapped together, he thought about kissing some sense into that anxious brain of hers.

"You're right." Her words were so soft, he wasn't sure she'd spoken them. "He's wonderful. Really awesome. But honestly…" She gave him a sharp if slightly tipsy look. "I've never said this to anyone, so you can't tell a soul."

He gave her a droll look. "Who am I going to tell?"

She stared him down for several seconds as if judging his sincerity. "Cross your heart?"

"Cross my heart," he repeated, making the motion against his chest.

"Okay." She bit her lip. "It's just that…sometimes I doubt

we're meant for each other."

"Really?"

"Yes. I know it's crazy," she murmured. "Especially since I can't afford for my software to be wrong."

Before he could respond, the lights overhead flickered. Her head whipped up toward the ceiling. "Thank God!" The elated expression on her face reminded him of a child watching fireworks go off. "We're finally going to get out of here," she squealed.

"Yeah…awesome." Matt swallowed hard. He should be happy, too. Why the hell wasn't he happy? He'd finally be out of this cramped elevator and away from this anxiety-ridden woman with her boyfriend issues. But instead, all he could do was bank down a strange sense of disappointment at the thought of her walking through those elevator doors and him never seeing her again.

He stood first then held out his hand to help her up. Her palm met his, and he tugged just as the elevator began to move again, causing them to lose their balance. His back slammed against the wall, and she fell into his arms.

"Nice catch," she said with a laugh, obviously still feeling the effects of the champagne.

Matt held on to her, his heart beating wildly. Having her in his arms ignited all kinds of thoughts, all kinds of feelings. Naughty thoughts. Good feelings. His gaze captured hers for a long moment until eventually her smiling face grew serious, too. Then his conscience tapped him on the shoulder.

What the hell do you think you're doing? it said. *You've both been drinking. And she has a boyfriend.*

He'd always hated his conscience.

"Matt?"

Matt didn't move. The elevator was going to open soon. They would be free to leave separately or leave together. There was still a choice. Growing up, he had always been the one to toe the line. Do what was right for everyone else in his life. But so help him, he didn't want to do that this time. Maybe it was the alcohol, but he wanted her. True, the woman had a boyfriend—a *neglectful* boyfriend—but still, there were rules for that sort of thing, weren't there? Like what if…

Screw it.

He kissed her.

And oh man, she tasted just as good as she smelled. He'd known she would. He pushed his tongue against hers, wanting to taste more, his blood pulsing through his veins making him drunk with need. It wasn't the alcohol in his system. He couldn't stop kissing her, her mouth, her smooth neck. She wasn't protesting. In fact, she grabbed his shirt and yanked, slowly running her shaking hands over his stomach. He wasn't sure who was going to go up in flames first. Nor did he care.

"Well, well, looks like we got here just in time, Sal."

Kennedy broke the kiss first and gave him a good shove back. Two amused-looking firefighters and a few hotel staff stood before them.

"Are you okay, miss?" one of them asked.

Matt glanced at Kennedy. She had regained her breath, but her face had gone stark white. Matt reached for her, but she was already backing away from him as if he had a bomb strapped to his chest.

"I'm fine," she told the paramedic in a shaky voice. "I—I just want to go back to my room. *Alone.*"

"Kennedy, wait." Matt stepped forward, about to follow her, but the other firefighter blocked his way, giving him a look that made him doubt he'd even get two yards before being tackled on the grounds of sexual harassment.

She gazed at him, her expression distraught, but didn't utter another word. Then she turned around and ran off toward the stairs.

Chapter Two

Six months later

Her fiancé was going to kill her.

Kennedy really liked the sound of that—not the killing part, mind you. The *fiancé* part. But still, things wouldn't be looking good on that end, either, if she didn't find the slip of paper he'd given her that had his mother's home address on it. She'd already asked Justin twice to give it to her. If she had to tell him she lost it again, he was going to think she didn't care enough about meeting his family. And honestly, that couldn't be further from the truth.

For some reason the address kept disappearing. Weird. She was usually so much more organized. She dropped down on her hands and knees for good measure and checked under her desk. Maybe it had fallen and gotten wedged under a table leg.

"Kennedy!" Mia shouted, marching into her office.

Kennedy's head shot up and smacked the top of the desk. "Ow!"

"There you are," her marketing assistant said, bending down. "Hey, what are you doing on the floor?"

She gently rubbed the small lump already growing on her scalp. "Checking up on the cleaning service, what else?" she grumbled.

"Oh." Mia wrinkled her nose. "You were?"

Kennedy rolled her eyes as she climbed into her chair. "*No*, not really. Although, make a note that the cleaners need to vacuum under my desk better. I saw a dust bunny condo nicer than my own down there."

Mia whipped out a small spiral tablet from her back pocket and jotted it down. "Will do, boss. Anything else?"

"Yeah, why were you shouting? Can't we at least pretend we're a professional operation around here?"

"Sorry, Ken," Mia said, worrying her lip. "I guess I'm nervous to be put in charge while you're away. I want to make sure there aren't any problems that could come up."

Kennedy smiled at her college friend and now second-in-command of her business. She didn't know how she'd function if she didn't have someone working for her who she could trust like she would family. Mia joined the operation a little more than a year ago, after a painful divorce left her in need of a job and one that was close to her son's preschool.

"It's only going to be two weeks," Kennedy reassured her, "and most of that time will be over the Christmas holidays. Everything will be fine."

Fine for now, she wanted to add, but didn't dare even breathe that thought.

She'd been on pins and needles ever since Match of the Day—a rival company—opened its doors a few months ago. Another escort/matchmaking company. Of all things! She'd figured most of her competition was online sites. But this company—headquartered in Boston as well—seemed to offer every type of service her company did. Even the name sounded similar. It made her blood boil just thinking about that. She'd worked so hard to get where she was, and now she had more people—including poor Mia—dependent on her.

Kennedy turned toward her window, which overlooked Boston Harbor, and rubbed her temples. Her matchmaking software and the marketing plan Mia and the new PR firm had come up with was scheduled to roll out on Valentine's Day. As her football-loving cousin would say, it was a Hail Mary play for her business. She hoped he was right about that.

"I suppose it won't be too long a vacation," Mia said. "But I don't want you to worry about a thing while you're gone. Just enjoy the holidays and that yummy fiancé of yours."

The mention of Justin had her spinning around. "You're right. Justin *is* yummy and great...*isn't* he?"

Mia nodded with a dreamy, far-off stare. "Totally. I'm ready for you to try that software out on me. I wouldn't mind being matched with a Justin of my own."

Kennedy laughed. "Soon enough. My tech guys are still making the final tweaks, and then we send it to the test group."

When Kennedy first developed her software, she figured the only logical thing to do was try it out on herself. When she had, the results suggested that one Justin Ellis would be perfect for her. So, after looking over his matchmaking application, she decided to call him up. After the initial meeting, something immediately clicked between them, and they began dating. Now, they were engaged, and in only a few days, she was finally going to meet his family. The investors she had spoken to at the Vegas conference seemed to love that aspect of her software presentation, since it showed that she was not only the founder of an up-and-coming company, but also a success story as well.

"Oh, sure," Mia said, flipping her long, dark hair off her shoulders. "Hog all the good-looking guys for yourself."

"I love how I show up when someone mentions good-looking men." Her cousin, Trent, stood in the doorway, one shoulder propped against the doorjamb and a devastating grin on his handsome face.

Kennedy rolled her eyes but couldn't suppress a grin. "Come on in, Mr. Modesty."

Mia's mouth formed a little *O* as her gaze followed Trent into the room. Mia had always had a little crush on Trent, even before her marriage. Although maybe *crush* was too banal a word. *Starstruck* would be a better term, considering Trent had been quite the football star back then.

Kennedy snapped her fingers in front of her friend's face to get her attention. "Was there anything else you needed to go over with me?"

Mia let a little sigh escape, never breaking her gaze from Trent's face. "Uh-uh."

Trent politely smiled, which was a mistake in Kennedy's opinion, because it sent Mia from minor crush to full-on infatuation mode in less than a second. Honestly, the poor woman had it bad for her cousin. But Trent was already taken—thanks to Kennedy—by a sweet girl named Maddie he'd met through her own Match Made Easy efforts.

Her then-client Maddie McCarthy desperately needed a date to bring to her sister's wedding and had come to Kennedy for help. But when her last escort wound up in the hospital, Kennedy had to ask Trent to pose as Maddie's boyfriend instead. It was a little rough going at first for them, since Trent and Maddie had a tumultuous high school past together, but they were able to put it aside and eventually started to fall for each other for real at the wedding. Maddie moved in with Trent last month, and their own wedding was scheduled for June.

Kennedy walked around her desk and gave Mia a none-too-light shove toward the door. "Down, girl," she said under her breath. "My cousin is already spoken for."

For the first time since Trent arrived, Mia looked at Kennedy and blinked. "What did you say?"

"I said it's hard to find a good haberdashery store." She gave her a few more light shoves until she was outside the door. "You should get on that for our male escorts."

"Oh, okay." Goofy grin back in place, Mia lifted her hand and sent her fingers lightly fluttering. "See ya around, Trent."

Before Trent could respond, Kennedy slammed the door in Mia's face.

Trent chuckled. "You're a little hard on your employees, don't you think?"

Kennedy harrumphed. "She's not an employee. Mia is practically family. Besides, she needed a good reality check. I can't have her fawning all over you when you're clearly an unavailable man." She started to walk back to her desk then stopped in her tracks. "You're still an unavailable man, right?"

He stared at her as if she'd declared football a non-sport. "If it was my choice, we would have eloped and been on our honeymoon by now. But Maddie wants a traditional wedding—like her sister had."

Kennedy smiled. "I don't blame her. I want the whole nine yards for my wedding to Justin, too."

"Gee, do you think Justin will free up his schedule long enough to actually make it to his own wedding?"

"Tee hee," she said, resuming her hunt for Justin's mom's address. "Don't sell your gyms and become a comedian. For your information, Justin is taking a whole two weeks off to spend with me at his family's place on Cape Fin Island. We're leaving tomorrow."

Trent's brow knit. "You won't be spending Christmas here with us?"

Kennedy realized this would be the first Christmas in several years that they wouldn't be spending together and felt a slight weight on her heart as a result. She and Trent were both only children and considered themselves each other's sibling—especially since neither of them had the kind of parents who could give them a model family life. "No, I'm sorry, Trent. I thought I told you. It was the only time Justin could get off from work. And I've never met his mom or family before."

"You've been engaged for four months and you've never met his mom?"

"We need to take a ferry to get to her house. It's not like we can get together at the drop of a hat. And with Justin's schedule…"

"Yeah, yeah, yeah. I know. He has a *big* important job."

Trent's sarcastic tone set her on edge. "I can't believe this. Are you actually *jealous* of Justin?"

He regarded her stonily. "Hardly."

She planted a fist on her hip. "Then what is your problem with him?"

"I don't know!" Trent flopped down in a chair in front of her desk and raked his hands through his hair. "There's no problem. *That's* the problem. He's friggin' perfect."

She laughed out loud. Especially with the way Trent's lips snarled when he choked out the word *perfect*. Little did he know his outburst was music to her ears. She'd been searching for that perfect person for so long. "You're being ridiculous, you know that, right?"

"Am I? It just doesn't seem natural. You were matched by a computer."

"You mean Mabel."

Trent grunted in disgust. "See? You even named your computer. This whole thing gets weirder by the minute."

"Oh? And I suppose meeting your fiancée by posing as a fake escort and pretending to be her wedding date to fool her family is perfectly normal in your book?"

Trent folded his arms. "As a matter of fact, in some states, yes."

Kennedy shook her head, far too amused at her cousin to stay annoyed with him. "Trent, dear, I appreciate your... concern. I really do. But you have to face two facts. One, Justin is perfect for me, and two, matchmaking is what I do. I bring people together by a sensible methodology for a long-term commitment. My software is going to make a lot of lonely people very happy. How can you find fault in that?"

Trent blew out a defeated breath. "I can't, really. It did a good job. You and Justin are two of a kind."

"Aha!" She grinned triumphantly. "I told you I'm a genius."

"I don't think I uttered the word *genius* anywhere in that statement."

She shrugged. "Doesn't matter. It's implied."

"Okay, *genius*," Trent said with a chuckle. "I'll miss you over Christmas, but I understand. Plus, if Justin can make you take a well-deserved break from work, then I'm even more for you and him being together."

"*Riiiight*. A break from work." Kennedy's grin froze as she nonchalantly kicked the home laptop she was planning on bringing with her under her desk and out of Trent's sight. Yes, she was guilty of being just as much of a workaholic as Justin, but to be honest, she hadn't really planned on working *that* much over the holiday. Just a little bit. After all, her company needed her, especially with all the new marketing rollouts happening in February. She still had to follow up with some potential investors, too. Plus, she loved Match Made Easy. It was bringing a lot of people true happiness, which was all she ever really wanted to do. She just wished she had developed it and her software a lot sooner. After seeing her mother go through five husbands and then five divorces, she realized that some people were not especially good at finding their soul mate and needed help.

Sometimes…*a lot* of help.

Kennedy decided to take it upon herself to do something about that, and her little business project in college eventually turned into an actual career. A career she'd do almost anything to protect from a flash-in-the-pan rival company.

Trent cocked his head. "Everything okay, Ken?"

She realized she was wringing her hands and suddenly dropped them. "I'm fine," she blurted. "Why?"

"I don't know. Just checking. Call it family intuition, but you seem worried. Nervous about meeting Justin's family?" He winked.

"Worried about that?" She smiled. "No, not at all."

In fact, with all the things happening to her business, meeting the Ellis family was the one thing she was the least concerned about. Thank goodness something in her life was going right.

* * *

Matthew Ellis loved wine—almost as much as he loved women. That in and of itself said something, because when he first took over the family winery almost eight years ago, he had been strictly a beer drinker.

After he set the bottle down, he picked up his glass and held the contents up to the light. This varietal was an experiment: his own unique blend of red zinfandel, syrah, and merlot. Inspecting it from the top and then from the side, he noted the color looked good. He held it under his nose. A nice aroma of cherry and mocha. He resisted the urge to high-five himself and instead gave it a few swirls in the glass. He tentatively took a sip, allowing air to seep through his teeth, adding to the flavors the grapes had created. His verdict: absolutely delicious.

He grabbed a spit bucket and expelled what was in his

mouth. As much as he would have loved to swallow, nine a.m. was a little early in the day for him. He'd only made a few cases as a trial run. He'd have to stash a bottle for himself and save it for a special occasion.

"Oh, Matthew, there you are," his mother said, smiling.

Barbara Ellis looked a little shaky as she entered the winery. Matt grew concerned and placed his wine glass down to rush over to her. Ever since she'd suffered a stroke a few months ago, he'd been worried sick about her. The doctors seemed to be confident that with the medications they'd put her on the chance of having another one was fairly slim. But Matt didn't like those odds. He'd already lost his dad to cancer. He wasn't about to take any chances with his mother.

He took hold of her arm, and she placed her hand over his. "Now, Matthew, you stop fussing with me. You're too young to be such a worrywart."

He kissed her temple and winked. "Face it. I'm an old soul, Mom."

"Yes, I do believe you are," she said, patting his cheek, "in some ways. Serious as a heart attack about wine and my health." She lifted her chin and sniffed. "Wish that would trickle into *other* areas of your life…"

"What's wrong with the other areas of my life?"

"The inside of your house looks like it belongs in a fraternity and don't get me started on those…those…women you seem to find. I've seen Victoria's Secret models wear more clothing," she huffed.

"Again, I have to ask what's wrong with those areas of my life?" He grinned.

"Matthew James Ellis, you know exactly what I'm talking about. Why can't you find a nice young girl like Justin did?"

Matt gritted his teeth at the mention of his brother. It seemed as if every time he and Justin were in the same room, they'd get into an argument over Justin's neglect of the family—particularly their mother—so it never failed that when his mom brought his name up in conversation, Matt became annoyed. Because of Justin's crazy work schedule, they hadn't spoken in more than a year. "How do you know Justin's girl is nice?"

"I…uh…" His mom flushed. "Well, I've seen a picture of her, and she looks very nice. And she had plenty of clothes on, too."

He shrugged. "I'll take your word for it."

"Well, you won't have to, because she and Justin are coming for Christmas," she said, clasping her hands in excitement.

Matt had to sit down for that news. "Christmas? Seriously? Justin is finally coming home?"

"Yes, isn't it wonderful?"

"Peachy."

"I don't like your attitude," his mother said, shaking a finger at him. "It's Christmas. We should all be together and put past grievances behind us."

"I couldn't agree with you more, and I believe I've made similar statements to you over the past…oh, five years. But he's always had some lame excuse. And it usually revolved around his work. He has his law degree on top of his business degree. He should find a way to sue the company he's working for under some indentured-servant labor law. Poor Caitlyn doesn't even know what her middle brother looks like anymore."

His mom clucked her tongue. "Justin is hardly an indentured servant. He only works so much because he wants to get ahead."

Matt walked over to the wine bar to get some water to cleanse his palate. He grabbed a glass for his mom, too. "You mean he wants to get a Bentley. And probably a condo in France, if he hasn't already gotten one of those."

"Oh, he's not as materialistic as you make him out to be. Besides, I think he's changed. Or at least, I feel someone is changing him," she added happily.

"Who, the girlfriend?" he said, taking a drink.

"No, the *fiancée*."

Matt swallowed so hard he began coughing and couldn't stop until his mom banged on his back a few times. "Justin… is…engaged?" he choked out, dabbing his watery eyes.

His mom gave him a satisfied smile. "Yes, and that isn't all."

Good grief, there's more? "What else?"

"Justin is bringing her to meet us when he comes home. Isn't that wonderful?"

Matt didn't say anything. He was still trying to digest the part about Justin getting married. He found it highly unlikely he'd had the time to meet anyone, let alone cultivate a decent relationship with the hours he put in at his job. Unless he met someone just as ambitious and selfish as he was. And if that were the case, Matt had to talk him out of it. He had almost married someone like that himself.

His mom placed a hand over his. "Matthew, I *want* this to be wonderful. Please say you'll go out of your way to forgive Justin and help make it a nice, memorable Christmas for me—and for your sister as well. Since your dad's passing and my health issues, it's just made me realize how short life is and how precious family is to me. We haven't all been together for so long. This is a chance to recapture some nice memories and maybe even make some new ones. What do you say?"

Matt met his mom's steady yet hopeful gaze and crumbled like a cookie. "You know when you put it that way, I damn well can't refuse." He leaned in and kissed her cheek.

She chuckled. "I know. I can always count on you."

"Maybe I should have been a mailman."

"In your next life, dear. Right now, you make a very

handsome and talented sommelier. Just like your father."

"Thanks, Mom."

His mom stood. "They'll be here in a few days, so I'm going to call the butcher and order a nice prime roast for Christmas dinner."

"Okay, but don't overdo it. After all, it's just family."

"Nonsense. We have to make this holiday special for Kennedy."

Matt froze. He hadn't heard that name since his trip out to Vegas almost six months ago. A rush of emotions generated through his system. "Did you say her name is Kennedy?"

"Yes, why?"

Yes, why, Matt? It's not like that was the one name he couldn't seem to forget after all these months. "What exactly does she do for a living?"

His mom shrugged. "I'm not sure if Justin ever mentioned that. But to be honest, ever since the stroke, my memory hasn't been what it was. What does it matter, dear? We'll all find out about her soon enough."

Matt nodded then watched his mom leave the tasting room. Hell, how many Kennedys were out there in this country? He'd bet hundreds. Thousands. But something had sparked—almost like hope—when he'd heard that name. He never forgot the pretty little redhead with the wide blue eyes and kissable mouth. But it didn't matter now anyway. She was long gone, and he was back in Massachusetts about to do what he always did: take care of the family. And that was about to include a potential new sister-in-law he hoped was not as selfish as his own ex-fiancée had turned out to be. He and his brother may have had their differences, but he still wanted Justin to be happy. Hell, someone in this family deserved to be.

Matt ran his hand through his hair as he eyed his glass of wine, wishing it was five o'clock.

Chapter Three

Kennedy stared out at the panoramic view of Cape Fin Island with longing. The ferry ride was only thirty minutes, but she couldn't wait to meet Justin's family.

Family.

The word filled her with giddiness. She had never had much of a traditional family life growing up. Her mom went through husbands like most people went through underwear. That meant being uprooted from her school and friends every time they moved to a new town. Sometimes it only meant moving to a new house. But it always meant a new stepdad. Then when things didn't work out, she and her mom would come back to Midship, Massachusetts.

At least *that* part of her life was consistent.

That and the relationship she had with her cousin, Trent. They had bonded over their miserable upbringings and remained close to this day. But still, it was no substitute for the stability of a real home. A real family. And now, finally, she was going to have it.

Justin sat down next to her and handed her a steaming

cup. "Here. I thought this would warm you up. The bay air can go right through you."

"Thank you, sweetie. You know how much I love hot chocolate."

He frowned. "You do? I'm sorry. I got you a hot apple cider. The same as me."

"My second favorite." She grinned and gave him a peck on the cheek before carefully taking a sip. Justin's thoughtfulness and the heated cider warmed her insides. She had been feeling a bit chilled ever since they boarded the ferry. The sky had a dull gray overcast, and the dark, giant ribbons of clouds looked as if they might open up and start snowing at any minute.

She laid her head on his shoulder. "This is going to be so perfect. You, me, your family. Do you think we'll make hot chocolate with tons of marshmallows and decorate the tree together?"

Justin chuckled as he pulled out his cell phone and started scrolling through emails. "Babe, you know I hate chocolate. And for all I know my mom could have the tree up and decorated already."

Hate chocolate?

Her head snapped upright. She studied Justin's bent-over head and wondered if she had misheard him. Who on earth hated chocolate? She was sure she would have remembered something like *that* in the eight and a half months they'd been dating. How could something like that be? It was like hating sleeping babies or…Santa. She supposed in the grand scheme of things it didn't matter. She was sure she could convert him with the special chocolate shortbread cookie recipe Maddie had given her.

"So, uh, your mom decorates early, huh?" she asked, trying to hide her disappointment at the chocolate revelation.

He shrugged. "I don't know. My dad always liked real

trees, so he would take us a few days before Christmas to pick one out. Now I don't know what she does."

"Don't know what she does? What did she do last time you were home?"

Justin still hadn't looked up. He continued scrolling through his email, which was beginning to bug her. "I haven't been home for Christmas in years. I just haven't had the time. You know, with work and all."

Kennedy frowned. She couldn't imagine not visiting family during the holidays even with work. Almost everybody got Christmas Day off—especially in his field, since the stock exchange wouldn't even be open. She had always looked forward to spending the holidays with her cousin, especially after her mom passed away a few years ago.

Justin finally looked up, sending her that sweet little-boy smile that always melted her insides. "Kennedy, you coming home with me after being gone so long is what's going to make this Christmas so much more special."

Aww...he was so sweet when he wanted to be. And forgiving. After the elevator "incident" in Las Vegas, she'd confessed everything to Justin about the accidental kiss she'd had with a stranger. Much to her relief, Justin had laughed it off.

"Babe, you were in Vegas. The place is crawling with creeps, so I bet that kind of stuff goes down all the time in elevators. The poor guy probably thought he had a shot with you, since you'd both had a few drinks and were alone. You were lucky that's all he tried."

Kennedy hadn't really thought of it that way, particularly since Matt didn't seem like that type of guy. But what did she really know about him anyway? Besides the fact that he'd have a gold medal if kissing were a competitive sport. Not that she dwelled on the kiss much or anything. She didn't need to when she had such a wonderful, understanding man like Justin in her life.

How lucky could a girl get? She leaned in to kiss him, but he'd turned his head and attention back to his phone. Her lips landed on his ear.

Cheeks flushed, she straightened and turned back to her cider. It had already cooled.

"Hey, Justin, let's stop off somewhere and get your mom some poinsettias. I feel bad coming empty-handed to dinner."

"Sure. I'll text her and let her know we'll be a little late."

Kennedy gazed back at the land as the ferry approached the dock and smiled to herself. She had a good feeling about these next few weeks. Christmas the way she'd always dreamed. She couldn't wait to meet Justin's family. Not only would his mom be there, but he had a sister and a brother as well—and she was going to make sure they absolutely loved her.

...

His mom checked the pot roast in the oven for the fourth time then set a hand on her hip. "Oh my goodness, I didn't even ask Justin if Kennedy ate meat."

Matt crawled out from under the sink and stood. "I'm sure Justin would have told you something as important as that, knowing you were making dinner for them."

Come to think of it, Matt wouldn't have bet the winery on a statement like that. Justin made snap decisions, and he often made them without thinking ahead, so, more often than not, they were *wrong* decisions. Not that Justin could be told that.

His sister, Caitlyn, sprang into the kitchen, her long blond hair pulled up in a ponytail so high it looked like it had sprouted from the top of her head. Caitlyn was a senior in high school, great at cross-country and very studious. She also had the maturity level of a thirty-three-year-old.

"Shouldn't they be here by now?" she asked, stealing a carrot from the vegetable tray.

"The ferry might be running late," Matt said, turning on the faucet and letting the water run a few seconds. He flipped on a switch and right on cue the garbage disposal started grinding. He flicked it off. "You're all set now, Mom. Feel free to shove as much garbage down the drain as you want."

His mom came over to him, towel in hand, and gave him a kiss on the cheek. "Thank you. I don't know what I'd do if you weren't around."

"Call a real plumber?" Caitlyn said with a cheeky grin.

His mom whipped the towel at her. "Hush, child. Do you know what that would have cost me? I don't need to call anyone while I have Matt. Your brother is a wiz at everything."

"Did you hear that? I'm a wiz." Matt made a show of posing and flexing his muscles at his mom's compliments, making his sister crack up. Although he exaggerated his own importance in jest, his mom on the other hand did not and, he was sure, meant every word. Maybe to her he was a wiz, and that's why she depended on him so much, especially since his dad had passed. Matt had automatically taken on the head of the family role, which was why he felt so extra protective and would do anything for them. They depended on him.

His mom chuckled. "Oh, stop clowning around and go change. You can't see your brother and his fiancée dressed like that."

Matt looked down at his jeans and wrinkled gray T-shirt. Aside from a little water stain down his right thigh, he thought he looked fine. "What's wrong with what I'm wearing? It's just family."

Caitlyn and his mom exchanged a look.

"Care to revise that *wiz* description, Mom?" Caitlyn asked, folding her arms. "Matt, you haven't even shaved. Don't you want to make a good impression?"

"I am not going home to change," he told them flatly. "And why do I need to make a good impression? She's not marrying *me*."

"Obviously not, looking like that," his mother commented.

Caitlyn shook her head. "Matt, have some class. Kennedy works in the city and is probably used to men who wear clothing that says *Esquire for Men*. You're wearing clothing that says *GQ for Rednecks*."

Matt waved a finger at her black turtleneck top and lacy short skirt. "And I believe you're wearing clothing that says too big for her britches."

She stuck out her tongue at him, reminding him she was still only eighteen—thank God—and grabbed another carrot stick.

The doorbell rang, and his mom and Caitlyn took off, saving him from any more emasculating discussions of his current attire. He preferred comfortable and casual. It was the way of life was on the island. And if that made him happy, he was doing it. Besides, he'd conformed enough in his life, hadn't he? It had cost him his job in New York and his fiancée. His family—and his brother's fiancée—was just going to have to deal with this minor stance on clothing choices.

From the kitchen, he heard his mom's escalating excitement at seeing Justin. As Matt casually made his way into the living room, a familiar voice spoke, which had the hairs on the back of his neck standing on end. He approached slowly.

The woman standing next to his brother looked familiar. *Very* familiar.

Familiar enough to have been pulled into his arms and kissed. He blinked a few times to clear his vision.

It can't be.

The woman from the elevator.

Holy crap and all that was damn near impossible to

imagine, he had kissed his brother's girlfriend. Correction: his brother's *fiancée*! The same fiancée who had expressed doubts that she and her boyfriend…his brother…should even be together.

Matt's blood ran cold as he stood there. What was she doing engaged to Justin if she had doubts back then?

His mom embraced Justin again while Kennedy smiled politely at his sister and shook her hand, then Kennedy stepped back as Justin and Caitlyn hugged. Eventually Kennedy's gaze traveled north to where he stood off in the background and…*bingo*. Their eyes met. Complete and total recognition. And if he didn't misread it, there was also complete and total fear in those beautiful blue eyes of hers.

Matt stonily gazed back. *That's right, sister. I don't know what kind of game you're playing with my brother, but I'm about to call an end to it.*

Justin took Kennedy by the hand and dragged her over to where he was. Matt clapped his brother on the back and gave him a hug. Their relationship had taken a hit ever since their father died, but it didn't mean he didn't love his brother or couldn't put his feelings aside, especially around the holidays. "Good to see you, man."

Justin looked good. Happy. Although Matt couldn't tell if it was the lifestyle he'd been leading or his newfound love that was causing the sudden elation. He hoped it wasn't the latter. He didn't trust this woman and would hate to have someone like her stringing his brother along for her own purposes.

Justin pulled back, grinning. "Good to see you, too, Matt. Looking dapper as ever," he said, gesturing to his T-shirt and jeans.

Caitlyn cleared her throat and sent him a *didn't-I-tell-you?* kind of grin.

Yeah, yeah. Tough noogies.

"I want you to meet my fiancée, Kennedy Pepperdine,"

Justin said, proudly pulling her to him.

Matt had to give the woman bonus points when it came to playing it cool, because she didn't hesitate one iota in schooling her features and holding out her hand to shake his. "Nice to meet you, Matt. Justin has told me so much about you."

Oh, this woman is good.

"Really? Wish I could say the same. Although you *do* look familiar now that I think about it," he added, enjoying seeing Kennedy's eyes widen.

Caitlyn took Justin's arm. "Come on, Just, I want to show you the magazine article I cut out about you. It's so cool," she added, leading him into the kitchen.

His mom walked over to Matt, looking happier than he'd seen her in years. "Matthew, look what Kennedy brought me. A lovely poinsettia," she said, holding up the plant. "Isn't she a sweetheart?"

Matt's gaze traveled back to Kennedy, who stood as stiff as a fireplace poker. "She's something, all right."

Kennedy bit her lip. "I, uh, left my briefcase with the luggage in the car. I'd better go and grab it. I don't want my laptop freezing."

"I'll go with you," Matt offered, enjoying how her cheeks drained of all color.

"No, no," she said, holding up a hand as if to keep him back. "Don't worry, I can handle it myself."

"I *insist*."

Kennedy's mouth opened as if to protest again, but fortunately for him, his mom intervened. "Yes, Matthew, be a gentleman and help Kennedy with her luggage. I'll go put the poinsettia on the table as a centerpiece."

She turned and walked off, leaving him alone with Kennedy for the first time since Vegas. Matt folded his arms, and Kennedy's complexion took on a greenish hue. For several moments, they just stood there in silence.

Kennedy was the first to cave. "Well…this is…this is kind of awkward."

Awkward. That word didn't seem to do the situation justice, but it was a start. Matt rested his thumbs in the front pockets of his jeans and regarded her closely. "I'm assuming the boyfriend issues you were having when I met you in Vegas involved Justin?"

She paused just a fraction of a second. So briefly that he would have missed it altogether if he had chosen to blink just then. "Yes."

Well, at least the woman was honest.

"Everything all magically resolved now?"

She frowned—actually had the nerve to look at him like he was out of his mind. "I wouldn't say magically resolved. Yes, we had some minor issues with our relationship, but we worked them out."

"Well, you certainly didn't kiss me like a woman who just had *minor* relationship issues."

"You know," she said, lowering her voice and jabbing her glasses back up her nose, "if I remember correctly, it was *you* who kissed *me*."

"And if *I* remember correctly, it was *you* who kissed *me back*."

She gasped. "I did not."

"Did, too"

"You grabbed me."

"You didn't push me away."

"I'd been drinking."

"Not that much."

Folding her arms, she stomped her foot. "I was under undue stress from being trapped in an elevator thousands of feet up in the air. And that kiss was so brief, I can't believe you're making such an issue out of it. I barely even remember it."

Oh, he remembered it all right. Unfortunately.

"Does Justin know you make a habit out of kissing strangers?"

"I could ask you the same question."

"It seems like a more honest fiancée would have mentioned that to him."

"How dare you assume I didn't tell him." She poked him in the chest. "Justin didn't think anything of it. Because it *wasn't* anything. And you have no right to judge me, especially when it was *your* fault." Another poke.

He narrowed his eyes. "Oh, believe me, I've already judged and handed down the verdict, honey. My brother deserves the best, and something tells me that isn't you."

Kennedy blinked, looking hurt and suddenly fragile, so much so that he wanted to offer up an apology, and probably would have if his mom hadn't come back into the room.

"Everything okay in here?" she asked, looking back and forth between them.

Kennedy turned and offered her up a brittle smile. "Yes, everything is great, Barbara. Thank you. Matt and I are just getting to know each other better. Tell Justin I'll be right there."

His mom looked uncertain for a moment, then nodded and went back to the kitchen.

Matt glanced at Kennedy's dejected face and sighed. She didn't look like a conniver, especially with her hair pulled back in a low ponytail and those purple-framed glasses slipping down her nose. She looked like a woman who hoped to make a good impression on her fiancé's family and, instead, got verbally attacked. He should have handled the situation differently. Kennedy wasn't Samantha. He didn't know why he would even compare her to his ex-fiancée, but maybe deep down inside he wanted to save his brother from the pain of making the kind of mistake he'd made.

"Look, sorry I went off about how you don't deserve my brother. I really don't know you well enough to say that yet."

Kennedy's head whipped up. *"Yet?"*

"I just mean you don't seem like his type."

"How do you know what his type is? From what I hear, you two have barely spoken in years."

"Well, I've known him a hell of a lot longer than you have."

Kennedy closed her mouth, looking as if she'd been slapped in the face. "Fine," she said quietly. "I guess we'll see about that, won't we?"

"Yeah, I guess *we* will."

"Don't bother with my bags," she told him pointedly. "For your information, Justin prefers his women self-sufficient." And with that, she flipped her ponytail back and walked out the front door.

Chapter Four

Kennedy pushed her mashed potatoes—which were absolutely delicious—around on her plate at least four more times before finally giving up and setting down her fork. It was no use. Her nerves were tightly wound. What were the odds that Justin's brother would be the same man she confessed her relationship problems to? The same man who'd kissed her?

Okay, she needed to calm down. *She* hadn't done one thing wrong. Maybe even by later tonight, she and Matt would be sharing a good laugh about it all.

She snuck a peek at him, sitting across the table from her. Matt's face was all scrunched up as if he smelled bad fish. His plate looked barely touched, too. He was on his third glass of wine and appeared to be having just as much difficulty getting through his meal as she was. Oh dear.

Have yourself a merry little Christmas…

She wished she'd never gotten on that stupid elevator when she was in Vegas. Wished she could have met Matt for the first time today and have her first meeting with Justin's family go perfectly. Like she wanted it to be. Like it was *supposed* to be.

Instead, Matt had acted so cold and said those hurtful things to her. Like somehow she was to blame for him grabbing and kissing her six months ago. *He* was the one who had the confessing to do. Even though she had already told Justin about the kiss, she wouldn't put it past Matt to make it look like it was her fault. So now she could only hope he'd forget about it and move on. After all, she had.

Mostly.

She cared deeply for Justin. They belonged together. Her software said so. His mother and sister had said so, too, many times over dinner, even. The only person who still seemed unconvinced was Matt.

Barbara pointed a fork at Kennedy's plate. "Are you feeling all right, dear? You hardly touched your dinner."

Justin swung an arm over Kennedy's shoulders and grinned. "She's probably already worried about fitting into her wedding gown," he said with a wink.

Kennedy gave them all a weak smile. "Yeah. Right. Never too soon to start worrying about that stuff." *And all* stuff: *failing business, mean future brother-in-law, whether or not I packed extra paper bags for my stress-induced asthma.* Just to name a few.

Her lungs *were* starting to feel a little tight…

"Oh, but my dear, you look wonderful already," Barbara assured her.

Justin gave Kennedy a quick kiss on the temple. "I couldn't agree more. I'm one lucky bastard."

"Language, dear." His mother frowned. "Your sister doesn't need to hear that kind of talk."

Caitlyn sighed. "Mom, I hear much worse in school. Actually, from Matt, too."

Barbara set down her fork and glared at Matt. "Matthew!"

He held up spread hands. "For the record, most of what I say is muttered under my breath. How was I supposed to know she has the ears of a bat?"

"Well, kindly mutter those words in your head from now on."

"Oh, don't worry. I will." Matt balled up his napkin and threw it at his sister. "You'll be happy to know that I'm muttering quite a few in my head right now."

"Mom!" Caitlyn yelled, deflecting his napkin. "Tell him to stop. He's messing up my hair."

"Well, fight back, then," Matt countered. "You're an Ellis."

"I can't fight back. There's nothing to combat. *You're* already such a mess," she said, batting her eyelashes.

"For the tenth time, I look *fine*," he said through his teeth.

Kennedy couldn't help it; a laugh bubbled up inside her and spewed out, earning her a glare of her own from Matt. But she didn't care. She was enjoying watching Justin's family—being a part of it—and seeing the love and playfulness among them. She could only pray Matt didn't blow this opportunity for her. A loving, stable family life was everything she had wanted for herself growing up but could never quite attain. Her mother would've had to stay married to a man for more than a year for that to happen.

Justin's cell phone went off, and like a candle being snuffed out, the energy of the room died and everyone focused on their food again. He pulled his phone out of his jeans pocket and looked at the screen.

"Oops, sorry," he said, standing up. "Gotta take this." Before Justin could leave the room, he was already addressing whoever was on the other end of the call.

Barbara shot a warning look to both Caitlyn and Matt before turning her attention to Kennedy. "My dear, I feel as if Justin has told me so little about you. What do you do again?"

"She owns a matchmaking company," Matt said.

Kennedy began to choke on her wine. Matt looked up with wide eyes as if he realized his mistake, too.

"How do *you* know that?" Caitlyn asked.

Matt cleared his throat. "Uh, Kennedy told me when we were in the living room."

"Yes! Right," Kennedy chimed in. "I told him in the living room. Today." Okay, she was babbling now, and her cheeks felt like they were two hundred degrees as everyone stared at her. "Uh, anyway, it started out as a small business project in college, but then it kind of took on a life of its own, and I decided to run with it. I employ twenty people right now, which includes staff and escorts, and we've been able to rent a nice office in downtown Boston." *For now, anyway*. Until she could find a way to combat their newest competitor if her software plan didn't pan out.

"That sounds wonderful," Barbara said. "I can't believe such a business can survive in this economy."

Kennedy put down her wine glass. "You would be surprised how much help people need with meeting other people nowadays. Everyone is busier than ever with work schedules. And nobody wants to hang out in a bar, hoping to meet Mr. or Mrs. Right. We can cut the time in half and bring people that much closer to their true love."

Matt snorted then shoved a forkful of meat into his mouth.

Barbara frowned at her son. "That is so true," she said, turning her attention back to Kennedy. "And how did you meet Justin?"

"Through my own company," she said, chuckling at herself. "Justin happened to apply to Match Made Easy, and at the time, I was testing out my newest matchmaking software. His name linked with mine when I added in all the data. So I decided to give him a call, and we hit it off right away. I think once we officially roll out that software to all our clients, it's going to bring happiness to a lot of people."

Barbara beamed. "Amazing. All from a computer program. Maybe you could help poor Matt here with finding a date."

"I don't need help finding a date." He directed his gaze toward Kennedy then gave her a slow lethal grin. "Believe me, I get *plenty* of dates on my own."

Kennedy's knees quivered, and she had to look away from those intense gray eyes. Yes, it would be fair to say she didn't have doubts about him getting plenty of dates.

"He's zero for one in relationships, though," Caitlyn added.

His mom nodded. "That ex-fiancée who shall remain nameless still makes my blood boil."

"Let's not go there, okay?" he said tightly.

Kennedy's eyebrow quirked. So cynical Matt Ellis had been engaged. Interesting…

His judgmental inquisition made much more sense now. She'd seen it a lot when she'd talked to clients with similar backgrounds. The man obviously had been burned. And burned badly.

Barbara dabbed her mouth delicately with her napkin. "It wouldn't hurt to try Kennedy's business, Matthew, and meet a woman you could share a future with."

"No offense to Kennedy's business, but using that bogus computer software to meet my perfect match seems ridiculous. And I'm not interested in meeting a future wife."

Kennedy squared her shoulders. "Hey! My software is not bogus. It has the potential to help a lot of lonely people out there. We're not just sticking people together. It's very scientific."

He snorted again. "I don't think so. Winemaking is scientific."

"Well, some people may think winemaking is ridiculous."

"You cannot compare the two. Besides, I'm selling an actual bottled product. You're selling a pipe dream."

A pipe dream?!

She immediately saw fire and crumpled up her napkin, throwing it down on her plate like a gauntlet. "What do you mean by *that*?"

Caitlyn popped out of her seat. "I'm getting my phone. This is Snapchat worthy."

"Sit down," her mother ordered.

Before Kennedy could further defend her software and company, Justin came walking back into the dining room wearing a troubled expression. "Hey, guys, I've got bad news."

I already know. Your brother is an ass, and we're stuck spending Christmas with him. What could possibly be worse news than that?

"I have to head back to Boston. Only for a few days." He looked down at Kennedy and sent her an apologetic shrug, stroking the back of her head. "I'll be back before you even miss me, babe."

That *was* bad news. She blinked.

Wait.

Miss you? He wasn't taking her with him?

"Oh, that's a shame, dear," his mother said. "Work again?"

"I'm afraid so, Mom. You know how it is when you're trying to vie your way up the company ladder."

"No, we don't know how it is," Matt said, sounding annoyed. "Explain to us why you have to leave your family *and* your fiancée five days before Christmas when you're supposed to be on vacation."

"Look, Matt, you don't understand. I have to make myself available whenever they need me. Show them I'm a company man. Besides, I really should be there to supervise this portfolio presentation if it's going to be done right. I'm sorry, but this shouldn't take too long. I'll definitely be here for Christmas. In the meantime, everyone can get to know Kennedy better."

Kennedy swallowed. *They can?*

Caitlyn bounced in her seat. "Ooh, Matt can take Kennedy and me Christmas tree shopping. That'll be fun."

Spending *any* time with Matt did not sound like her idea of fun. The man was as serious as a brain hemorrhage. "Uh, Justin," Kennedy said, finally finding her voice, "maybe I should head back with you, since you're only going to be a few days."

Barbara stood, taking her plate and then Kennedy's. "Nonsense. Justin's right. There's no need for you to leave. It'll be nice to spend some quality one-on-one time with you. After all, you're going to be a daughter to me soon."

Kennedy's heart lifted a fraction at the word *daughter*. Justin's mom was so kind. Maybe this would be a good thing. It would be nice getting to know her and Caitlyn better. And if she was spending quality time with them, there was less of a chance of having to see Matt.

Justin beamed at his mom. "You're the best. I'm going to have to leave on the first ferry tomorrow morning."

Barbara nodded. "Then after breakfast, Matt can take Kennedy over to the winery with him and show her around."

Matt shifted in his seat then cleared his throat. "Uh, Mom, I don't think Kennedy will be interested in the winery."

"Of course she would, and I think you two might get a better appreciation of each other's work this way, too. Besides, the grounds are beautiful, especially now, since it's decorated for the holidays. You'll love it," she assured her.

Spend the morning with Matt? Oy. She glanced at Matt's stony expression. Not exactly the face for Enthusiasm "R" Us, that's for sure. She was hardly doing cartwheels, either. But Barbara seemed adamant about it. Kennedy didn't see any way out—without the good fortune of sudden illness or possibly death.

She could only be so lucky.

"Wonderful. Now that that's settled," Barbara said brightly, "who wants pie?"

• • •

The next morning Kennedy tiptoed into Justin's bedroom, hoping to get in a little snuggle time before he had to leave, but she found him showered and all ready to go. Had he even planned to wake her to say good-bye?

"I miss you already," she said, wrapping her arms around his waist.

Justin closed his laptop case with a final snap. "You are the most understanding fiancée in the whole world." He kissed her then walked to the dresser and picked up his watch.

Kennedy sat on his already-made bed and tried to smile. She didn't feel like the most understanding fiancée at the moment. In fact, she was pretty sure she was a heartbeat away from grabbing his legs and begging him not to go. Not that she felt funny staying alone in his mother's house with his sister. They were more than welcoming and kind. Kennedy worried more about Matt. He obviously didn't care for her or what she did for a living, and without Justin around, she felt he would only make her stay here even more uncomfortable and possibly ruin her relationship with the rest of the family.

"Are you sure it will only take two days?" she asked. She glanced at the digital clock on the nightstand. By her estimation, it would actually take forty-six hours until he returned. That actually wasn't so bad.

Justin walked over and sat down next to her. Placing his hand on hers, he leaned in. "Babe, I promise you, as soon as I'm done I will rush back here to spend the rest of my holiday vacation with you. Don't you know it tears me apart to be away from you, too?"

She snuggled closer to him. "It does?"

"Yeah. And once I get back, we'll do all the fun things you want to do."

"Really? Like decorate the tree and have hot chocolate with marshmallows?"

He sighed dramatically. "Yes. Even the hot chocolate part. And you know how I feel about chocolate."

"Oh, Justin. You are just the perfect fiancé," she said, wrapping her arms around his neck and pulling him in for a kiss.

True, Kennedy had had some doubts about their relationship when she'd been in Vegas, but once she'd returned home, she and Justin had a long talk about each other's wants and needs. He had promised her that he'd be mindful of not putting work ahead of their relationship. And here he was showing her that he was conscious of it. So he really was trying. "Thank you for making this Christmas the best one ever for me," she added, smiling into his eyes.

He chuckled. "Christmas hasn't even come yet and you're thanking me already? Gee, I can't wait until you see the real gift I got you."

"The only gift I need is you back here with me for Christmas."

"You got it, babe." Then he kissed her again, and knowing this was their final good-bye, his mouth lingered on hers for longer than usual.

"Ugh, at least have the courtesy to shut the door. I'd hoped you guys would have gotten this out of the way by now," Matt said from the doorway.

Justin pulled back and grinned at his brother. "If you had a fiancée who looked like this, you wouldn't be so quick to be done, either." He stood and grabbed his bag. "What are you doing here at the house so early anyway?"

"I'm heading over to the winery in a bit, and Mom gave me strict orders to entertain Kennedy for the morning, so here I am." With outspread arms, he cocked an eyebrow at her. "Ready, future sis?"

Kennedy took off her glasses and rubbed her head. How had she forgotten about that? She glanced at the clock again. Only forty-five hours and forty-five minutes until Justin would be back. She could do this. She just had to channel her inner Mother Teresa.

Justin shook Matt's hand. "Thanks for holding down the fort, Matt."

"I usually do," Matt muttered.

"Well…yeah." Justin ran a hand through his spiky blond hair and sighed. "I still appreciate it."

"Call me," Kennedy added. She had a feeling she'd need a lifeline more than ever.

Justin gave her a funny look. "I always call you when I'm away, babe."

Well, actually, you don't. Hence the reminder. But she wisely kept that to herself. He'd promised he would not be neglectful anymore, so she had to give him the courtesy of a fresh slate.

"Have fun at the winery, you two," Justin said with a quick wave. "Wish I could stay, but you know how it is, duty calls and all that jazz."

Justin winked at her then grabbed his suitcase and walked out, leaving her suddenly feeling very lost and very alone. Something she hadn't felt with this much intensity since her mother passed away.

The room went silent, and she cautiously peered at Matt. He remained outside the bedroom door, staring at her like someone who just stepped foot onto a *Walking Dead* episode. That made her decision to put them both out of their misery that much easier.

"Look, Matt, you don't have to do this. I can entertain myself for the morning." She could check in with Mia at work, maybe even answer the hundreds of emails that were probably waiting for her. She thought about her laptop longingly.

He shook his head. "Caitlyn is at school, and if you're here, my mom will feel the obligation to dote on you when she really should be taking it easy."

"Is everything okay?"

"I'm surprised Justin didn't mention it, but she had a stroke a few months back."

Kennedy bit her lip. Justin never said a word to her about that. But maybe he didn't want her to worry about coming to stay there for the holidays.

"Anyway," Matt said, "it's not a big deal to bring you with me. Like my mom said, it's really pretty this time of year, and the tasting room looks festive, too. I'm sure you'll enjoy seeing it."

Kennedy could barely believe cordial words were finally coming out of Matt's mouth. Maybe there was some hope for them yet.

"Okay. That's nice of you."

He shrugged. "I'm a nice guy."

She wanted to point out that his statement was a tad flawed, but he seemed to be making amends over his past actions toward her, so she gave in to a smile.

Matt's eyes fell to her lips for a moment, and then he took an abrupt step back. "Well, don't read too much into it," he murmured as he turned away. "You know how it is, duty calls and all that jazz."

Chapter Five

Matt scratched his head as he walked into the kitchen. He knew Justin could be blind to everything going on around him, but damn if he could understand how his little brother could leave his beautiful fiancée behind for any amount of time on account of work. Matt had taken care of Justin and the family since their father had died, making sure the winery was still viable and his mom could still pay for Justin's education. Even made a few phone calls to old business contacts and got Justin an interview at the firm where he was currently employed. And now Matt was left taking care of things for Justin again — which meant the redhead upstairs wearing Snoopy pajamas. A redhead Matt couldn't help picturing *out* of those Snoopy pajamas.

Dammit. He wasn't supposed to be attracted to his brother's fiancée. But that didn't seem to change the fact that he was.

He took out his phone and glanced at the time. It wasn't even nine a.m. and it was already shaping up to be a very long day.

"Oh, Matthew, you're here early." His mother shuffled into the kitchen in her pink slippers and bathrobe, brushing a light kiss on his cheek. "Did Justin leave already?"

"Yeah, he left," he grumbled. *Without his fiancée.* Although he did have to give Kennedy major points for the lack of drama about it. In fact, she took Justin leaving her behind with more understanding than he would have shown.

"Do you want some breakfast?"

"No fussing, Mom. Once Kennedy gets ready, we'll stop at Nonna's Breads and pick up something. You just relax."

His mom shook a finger at him. "You're mothering again. That's supposed to be my job."

"Well, now it's mine. And apparently, babysitting has been added to my resume as well."

"I hardly think you could call being brotherly and showing Kennedy around while Justin is away 'babysitting.' I told you, be nice. No more ribbing about her company."

"You mean the one that sells true love at the click of a button? *That* company?"

The sarcasm wasn't lost on his mother, and she frowned. "Now, Matthew. I don't know why you're being so hard on her, but whether you like it or not, she's going to be family soon. Give her a chance. For the first time in a long time, it really feels like Christmas with everyone all together."

"But everyone *isn't* together," he reminded her. "Justin left."

"He'll be back. You'll see."

Matt laid the odds at four to one on Justin making it back in time for Christmas day, but didn't want to burst his mom's bubble. Instead, he asked, "What do we really know about Kennedy anyway?"

"What do you mean?"

What do I mean?

For some reason, Kennedy and his brother just didn't

seem to fit together in his mind. Kennedy was obviously pretty. She also happened to be a clever businesswoman, even if he didn't happen to think much of her business. Back in college, Justin had girlfriends who were self-absorbed and served no real purpose other than being mere arm decoration. "What exactly do she and Justin have in common?"

His mom patted his cheek as if she were calming a petulant two-year-old. "If you're so intent on finding out the answer, you can ask her that yourself."

"Ask me *what* yourself?"

Kennedy stood in the entryway of the kitchen, all wide-eyed and perky with her blazing red hair curling over her shoulders. In her green wool coat and matching knit hat and mittens, she looked like she could be going for a job interview at Santa's workshop.

And be hired in less than two minutes flat.

"What do you and Justin have in common?" he blurted.

She blinked. "Uh, lots of things."

"Name one."

"Don't mind Matthew, dear," his mom said with a scowl aimed his way. "He's always a Grumpy Gus before breakfast. Did you sleep well?"

"Yes, thank you. I'm actually used to sleeping in strange beds."

Matt folded his arms. "And what the *hell* is that supposed to mean?"

"Language," his mother scolded.

Kennedy's pretty face scrunched together and the red-framed glasses she wore slid down her nose. "I just mean that my mom and I moved around a lot when I was younger. I've had five stepdads in my life—almost six—but then she got breast cancer and...well, it was just the two of us when she passed away last year."

"Oh, I'm sorry, hon." His mom walked over and gave her

a hug. "That must have been hard on you."

"It's fine," she said into his mom's shoulder, but when she pulled back, Matt noted that tears clung to her eyes. "My cousin, Trent, helped me a lot. But I have to admit, it's really nice to be part of a traditional family again."

Matt let his arms hang, feeling like a fool. What was the matter with him? He'd been acting like an ass ever since Kennedy stepped foot into his family's house. His mom was right. He needed to be nice—in a very brotherly and platonic way—and give the woman a chance.

Matt walked up to them and laid a hand on her shoulder. "Hey, Kennedy, we should get going now. Since you're practically family and all, it's probably time to show you around."

"That would be great." Kennedy's smile was alive with delight, and like a swift punch to the gut, it left him temporarily speechless.

He turned to grab his jacket and drew in a deep breath. "Okay then. We'll stop for coffee on the way. You haven't lived until you had Nonna's chocolate croissants."

"You like chocolate?"

Her startled expression made him chuckle. "Of course I do. Only deranged lunatics without taste buds don't like chocolate. Why?"

She bit her lip, then with a dazed expression made her way to the back door. "Oh, uh, no reason."

· · ·

Kennedy immediately decided that Cape Fin Island was a darling town. Gingerbread-style homes lined up along the bay with their window boxes filled with assorted evergreen branches and pinecones. Street lamps were adorned with garland and bows, and traditional Christmas music played through outside speakers in the downtown area. Everything looked perfect and exactly how she hoped it would be. Matt was almost being cordial to her as well. Bonus. All that was needed to top this scene was a little snow.

"It's so adorable," she sighed. When Matt didn't say anything, she glanced over at him.

His dark hair was slightly disheveled from the cold, brisk wind. He hadn't bothered shaving, but she still noticed a tiny scar on his stubbly cheek. In his work boots and jeans, he looked more like a construction worker than a winemaker. Not that he didn't wear the tall, dark, and rugged look well. He wore it *extremely* well. It was a good thing Matt was the furthest thing from her type. He was just an overgrown kid, unlike Justin, who was ambitious and also serious about settling down.

She turned toward the window again. They passed an artisan soap store. Kennedy thought his mother might enjoy some fragrant skin care supplies. "I'd love to go Christmas shopping here this week."

Matt parallel parked his pickup truck then shut off the engine. "Caitlyn mentioned that. Maybe once she gets home from school, you guys can go." He opened the truck door and got out. "I'm just the supplier of coffee."

Kennedy saw they were in front of a bakery called Nonna's that had a huge lit-up coffee mug in the window. "And supplier of chocolate baked goods?" she asked with a grin.

"Of course." He grinned back and opened the door for her to pass. "Can't let you taste wine on an empty stomach, now can I?"

Kennedy walked in, and her nostrils were filled with a scent that could only be described as heaven-on-speed-with-a-double-shot-of-espresso. Her knees even gave a little wobble. "Oh, Lord, they need to bottle this smell."

Matt chuckled. "I'm sure many have tried."

An attractive brunette with hair in a short pixie-style haircut came out of the back room carrying a tray of cinnamon buns. "Matt!" she cried. "You're late. But I managed to save you a couple of your favorites, only because you're so cute." She held up a white paper bag and dangled it out in front of her. "It wasn't easy, either. Mr. Jenkins almost had a hissy fit right in the middle of the seven o'clock slam until I gave him a slice of crumb cake on the house."

"Patty, you are a goddess among bakers," he told her, taking the bag and peeking into it.

She waved his compliment away. "Oh, please. Tell me something I don't know. But send me a bottle of your best cabernet, and then we can call it even. Maybe."

"Anything for you."

The brunette blushed then looked past Matt's shoulder and smiled. "Hi," she said to Kennedy. "May I help you?"

Matt shook his head. "Actually, she's with me."

Patty raised her eyebrows. "Why, Matt Ellis, did you actually bring a date to my bakery? I'm not sure if I'm flattered for myself or offended for her."

"Oh, no, we're not together," Kennedy blurted. "He's… We're just here…together."

"What Kennedy means to say is she's Justin's fiancée."

Patty gaped. "Holy snickerdoodles! Justin is getting married?" She came around the counter and wrapped her arms around Kennedy like a boa constrictor. "It's so nice to meet you. Why am I just hearing about this now? Ohmygosh, and why was I not invited to the party?"

Matt rolled his eyes. "Calm down, Patty. There was no party. In fact, Justin kind of sprung it on us only recently."

Kennedy tried to brush off the disappointment she felt at Justin not telling his family and friends about their engagement sooner. After all, with his work schedule, it was probably very hard to find the time to make a big announcement and do it properly. But still, a *little* party might have been nice…

"Do you know Justin well?" Kennedy asked.

"We all went to high school together, although he was a freshman when Matt and I were seniors. Those were the best times. Remember graduation night, Matt?" Patty gave Matt an appreciative wink, and Kennedy had to wonder if they were an item back then.

"Yeah, yeah, I remember," he murmured. Matt scowled and pulled a ten out of his wallet then set it on the counter. "This is for the pastries and two coffees. Keep the rest. See ya around." He quickly turned away and headed for the coffee bar.

Kennedy smiled at Patty. "It was nice to meet you. Maybe we'll see each other again while I'm in town."

"Hope so. And bring that fiancé of yours. I haven't seen Justin in years."

"I will. Thanks."

Kennedy scanned the room. Matt had found a table in the corner of the shop and already poured a coffee for her as well. His abrupt departure from Patty's conversation was strange—even by Matt's standards. She walked over to him, noting a shift in Matt's mood—the hunched shoulders and brooding Heathcliff-like stare into his coffee. Unfortunately, he wore "tortured hero" almost as well as the construction-worker look.

As soon as she sat down, Matt wanted her to try her croissant. He hadn't said anything in words, mind you—merely pointed and grunted—but she was beginning to understand his caveman-like tendencies the more time she spent in his presence.

She bit into it and almost swooned from sheer pleasure. The croissant was buttery with just the right amount of sweet. The chocolate center was still slightly warm and melted.

Patty—bless her heart—really was a bakery goddess. Kennedy hesitated before swallowing, unwilling to let the flavor leave her tongue quite yet. How could Justin not love this?

Still savoring the taste, she added cream to her coffee then picked up a sugar packet. Matt still hadn't said a word, looking deep in thought. Curiosity got the better of her.

She cleared her throat, flicking an imaginary speck of lint from her wool coat. "So… Patty seems nice."

"Yup." He took a long sip of his coffee.

"She seems to like you."

"Patty likes all her regular customers."

"Maybe. But there might be something more to it than that. Did you guys ever date in high school?"

He finally glanced up, a faint twinkle in the depths of his gray eyes. "Are you matchmaking, Kennedy?"

Ha! She wished she were matchmaking. And she totally should have been. It was her business to help people find true happiness—especially her single future brother-in-law. Instead, she was just part curious and part feeling something else altogether ridiculous—like a tinge of jealousy. Or possibly hyperglycemia from scarfing down her chocolate croissant.

She shrugged. "I can't help it," she lied. "It's my calling."

"Well, there's a slight flaw in your efforts, and that would be her husband."

"Oh." Patty was married. She sat back and took a breath. That was nice. She was beginning to like her more and more.

"Look, if you want to know something, why don't you just come right out and ask?" he told her.

She blushed at the fact that he could read her motives so easily. Justin wasn't nearly so observant. "Well, you looked kind of upset when Patty mentioned graduation night. I thought maybe—I don't now—there might have been something that had gone on between you two."

He sighed. "No. She's just remembering the fun we all

had that night celebrating. And it *was* a lot of fun. I also met my future fiancée that night."

"You did? How?"

"Samantha and Patty are cousins. Sam came down from Peabody for Patty's graduation. We just clicked, you know? Even found out we were going to the same college in Boston. We were together the whole four years, so when we were seniors, we got engaged."

She bit her lip. "Can I ask what happened?"

"Yeah, my dad died. And my mom needed me. Had a job with Anchor Capital Investments all lined up and everything, but I had to leave it behind and come back home to help my mom run the winery. It would have absolutely killed her to have us sell and lose that part of my dad, too. Samantha didn't quite understand that at first, or maybe she hoped it was only going to be temporary, but either way, she didn't want to give up her job in the city to be with me. In the end, we just couldn't make it work."

Kennedy sat back as she considered this. Maybe Matt wasn't the overgrown child she thought he was, but merely a person who didn't have the time to worry about his own wants when he was taking care of his family's needs first.

"Where was Justin throughout all this?" she asked.

"Just got accepted to Fordham University. At the time it was probably good for him to be away, while Mom and I tried to figure out what we were doing with the winery."

She reached for his hand. "I'm really sorry about your dad and that things didn't work out with your engagement."

"Yeah, I was sorry, too. It was hard to realize the person you fell in love with wasn't the same person anymore. But I'm sure it would have been much worse if Sam and I found that out after we had already gotten married."

Kennedy listened with rising dismay. She knew full well what he was talking about, having lived through her mother's various broken marriages. Her mom always let her feelings rule over her head. If Kennedy had learned one thing from her mom, it was that feelings were fickle, and based on Kennedy's prior relationships before Justin, she had been headed on a path that mirrored her mother's.

Well, that wasn't going to happen. Thank goodness for her matchmaking software. Kennedy would never end up like her mom—with various heartbreaks and ultimately alone. No. Kennedy would go into a relationship with more scrutiny and care, weighing everything in her mind just so. It had to be perfect and orderly. Maybe she didn't trust her own instincts in finding her soul mate, but she had the utmost confidence in her company to help guide her. Justin was the man for her.

She was almost sure of it.

Kennedy cocked her head. "Did you ever have doubts about Samantha before you proposed? Doubts about getting married?"

"No."

She let out a deep, pent-up breath. That was sort of good to know. Maybe the few doubts she had about Justin were just her being thoughtful and extra cautious. A trait she was sure Justin appreciated about her.

"However…"

Her spirits began to sink. "However, what?" she asked.

"There was one person who did try to talk me out of marrying Sam." He paused. "Justin."

She blinked. "He did?"

"Yeah, but I figured, what did he know about relationships? He was only in his first year of college and had the most superficial taste in girls. Uh, no offense."

"None taken."

"Anyway, if I was a little hard on you before, it may have something to do with that. I kind of owe him. Plus, I don't want him to make the same mistake I did."

She straightened in her seat and met his gaze directly. "He won't."

Matt's gaze fell onto her hand, which was still on top of his, and a vaguely sensuous moment passed between them. Her face on fire, she pulled her hand away and dropped it onto her lap.

"Good," he said briskly. He stood and tossed his empty coffee cup in the trashcan with more effort than was needed. "If you're sure about Justin, then I'm sure."

She nodded. But something was off. She couldn't quite describe what. Matt's assurance about her and Justin being together should have brought her comfort, but for some reason his words felt more like a slap in the face.

Chapter Six

"These wines have all finished fermenting," Matt explained as he led her down the steps into the wine cellar. "And last month we bottled several wines from the 2015 vintage."

Kennedy couldn't see his face but could hear the animation in his voice as he talked about what was essentially his father's legacy. She understood how he felt; it mirrored her own pride whenever she talked about Match Made Easy.

There was a sink in the far corner of the room. Matt went over to it and picked up what looked like a baster and began rinsing it out. After he dried it, he turned around, holding it in the air. "This is by far my favorite thing to do."

"Cook a turkey?" she asked with a cheeky grin.

He chuckled. "No, taste wine. Wines evolve daily, so I love to see what's going on first thing in the morning with them. It sets the tone for my day." Walking over to one of the large barrels, he popped off the top cork and inserted the baster into the hole. He then removed it and squeezed a small sample into each of their wine glasses.

He held up his glass and swirled the wine around in

it. Matt looked so serious and intent, she had a hard time coming to terms with this side of him. He generally appeared lackadaisical to her in his attitude as well as his dress.

"What are we about to taste?" she asked.

"Pinot noir."

"Oooh, that's my favorite."

He grinned. "Mine too. It's actually one of the hardest varieties to make and really do it well. Maybe that's what puts it ahead of the other grapes for me. I like a challenge."

There was a gleam in his eye as he said the word *challenge*. Or maybe it was her imagination. Either way, standing so close to him, her senses began to swim, and she had to look away to keep her stupid body's response in check.

He's going to be family, she reminded herself firmly. "Um, so what's Justin's favorite wine?"

Matt cocked an eyebrow. "Isn't that something you should already know about your future husband?"

Ohmygosh. He was right. Why *didn't* she know that about Justin?

Her stomach clenched. "I—well, he— "

"Relax, Kennedy. I wasn't trying to put you on the spot. As far as I remember, Justin always loved bold cabernets. But tastes change. You'll have to find out before your wedding so we can make sure we can supply enough. After all, it wouldn't be a wedding without Ellis Estates wine, right?"

She let out a relieved smile. "Right. I'll be sure to find out." She raised her glass to her lips, but Matt placed a hand on her arm, stopping her from tasting it.

"Wait," he urged. "You're missing the epiphany."

"I'm missing the wine in my mouth."

He sighed. "There's a whole process to enjoying wine. For example, look at the color. What do you see?"

To pacify him, she held the glass up to the light. "I definitely see red."

"All right, smart ass, I can see my tutoring efforts are going out the window with you. Just go ahead and taste it."

"Finally." Grinning, she took a delicate mouthful. "Oh, Matt, it's delicious."

He shared her smile. "It is. Normally, I'd spit it out, but it's just too good. This one is going to be big." Matt set his glass down and re-plugged the barrel, looking pleased with himself.

"Seems like you really enjoy your job."

"I do. *Now.* It took a while. When I was younger, I rebelled and was a total beer guy. Funny how things work out, though. I never in a million years planned on taking over the winery. Thought it was going to be my parents' thing but now, I can't really see myself being anywhere else or even doing Justin's job."

Kennedy couldn't see Matt doing anything else, either. Not that she thought it was such a bad thing. Matt had his family close by and everyone in town knew him and his wines. There was a certain simplicity and familiarity to living and working in a small town that had Kennedy even a bit envious. Growing up, she'd never stayed in one town long enough to develop that kind of routine. Things were definitely going to change for the better once she married Justin. They'd buy a house in the suburbs of Boston, have a family, grow some roots. Everything would be perfect. Just like she always wanted.

Matt motioned to the stairs with his chin. "Come on. I'll show you the tasting room."

Kennedy followed him back up the steps. The tasting room had a long bar with a granite top. Dark leather barstools were evenly spread along the length of it. Wood built-ins with various bottle of wines outlined the wall behind the bar. On the left side of the room, a stone fireplace took up the entire wall where the fire was lit and crackling. A huge wreath hung above the mantel and a large Christmas tree decorated with garland made of cork. The room was elegant yet homey at the same time.

"Oh, this is lovely," Kennedy remarked, checking out the view of the vineyard from the glass wall behind them. "I can totally see events being held here."

"Well, that is part of the future plan. Right now I'm working some things out with the Chamber of Commerce and seeing if we can plan festivities to bring tourists into town all year long and not just the summer."

Kennedy's mind began to buzz with an idea that could potentially help both of them. "I'd love to hold a few mixers here for Match Made Easy. We have clientele all over the state and some might be interested in coming here to meet potential dates, and then make a weekend getaway out of it."

He held up a hand. "Wait. You want to hold your little matchmaking cotillions *here*?"

She planted a hand on her hip. "They're cocktail parties. I constantly have to think of innovative ways to keep my company fresh, too, you know. In fact, I already have some competition on my heels."

"Wow, there's a bigger market of lonely unmarried cat ladies than I originally thought."

She punched him in the arm. "I'm serious. I can even see an acoustic guitar player being in the corner there. Honestly, what do you think about us working together on this?"

"Hmm…" He scratched his chin. "You mean like a partnership?"

"Well, yes. If you can stand having to deal with me more often. I know you haven't exactly been waiting to sign up as the president of my fan club."

He sighed. "That's not true, Kennedy. You're not half bad. In fact, I guess you're okay, sort of, maybe."

"I'll try not to let that go to my head," she said dryly, making him laugh.

An older man bundled up in winter layers came in and smiled. "Oh, Matt, I wasn't expecting to see you here. I figured you'd be out in the vineyard pruning."

Matt walked over and shook the man's hand. "I'm a little behind schedule. Jim, this is Kennedy Pepperdine. I've been giving her the grand tour of Ellis Estates."

"Nice to meet you," Jim said, taking off his hat.

"Jim runs our tasting room here in the winter months during the afternoon. He also helps me wash and clean some of the equipment in the cellar, which is always a process. He knew my dad back in the day."

Jim nodded. "I did. He was a fine man, and I can tell you, miss, that Matt here is just as fine a man. You can't do better."

Kennedy flinched. "Oh, no. Matt and I aren't dating... No, in fact, I'm *engaged* to Matt's brother, Justin."

Jim sized her up with a quick drop of a glance then exchanged an odd look with Matt. "Ah, I see. Well, congrats." He rubbed his hands together briskly then began to unbutton his coat. "Well, I'd better get a move on. Don't want the boss to get sore." He winked. "Good meeting you, miss."

"See ya, Jim." Matt took hold of Kennedy's arm and ushered her out the front door.

The bitter cold air hit her in the face like a snowball, and she reached for the hat she'd slipped into her coat pocket. "What was that look Jim gave you when I mentioned being Justin's fiancée?"

"What?" Matt breathed into his fist to warm up his hands. "There was no look."

He picked up his gait, and she stumbled a bit to keep up. "Are you sure? Because I could have sworn I saw a look."

"Nope. No look." He stopped once he got to where his truck was parked then looked back at her. "Although if there *was* a look given—"

"I knew it!"

"It might be because he noticed that you're not wearing an engagement ring."

"An engagement ring?" Kennedy blinked, and her right hand covered her left as if she suddenly expected to find one on her finger. "Oh. Um, Justin proposed to me without a ring. He said he didn't want to surprise me with something I'd probably return."

Although she would never have done such a thing. She would have loved and cherished *anything* Justin would have presented to her.

"He wants to shop for a ring together, which is very logical. It's just that…we haven't had the time yet." More like *he* hadn't had the time yet. But Kennedy had hoped that since they had finally taken some time off together, they could shop for one here in town.

Matt shoved his hands in his pockets. "I didn't ask for an explanation."

"Oh, I know. But in case, you know, your mom or anyone else asks…" She shivered and dipped her head as the wind picked up.

Without warning, Matt reached out and began wrapping her scarf more securely around her neck. They stood there, gazes locked for a long moment.

"Don't want you to be sick for Christmas," he murmured.

Her heart thundered in her ears. Not a good reaction to have to such a simple gesture, so she quickly backed away. "Um, thanks."

Matt looked up at the sky. "Feels like it could snow."

"Oh, I don't think so. Justin and I double-checked the forecast before we left. Definitely no snow in sight."

He sent her a crooked smile. "Are you always so sure of computers and technology? I tend to have pretty good gut feelings about these kinds of things."

"Oh, really?"

"Really."

"Bet on it?"

He laughed. "Oh, I see what's going on," he said, shaking a finger at her. "If I'm wrong, then you want to have a few of your company cocktail parties at the winery, am I right?"

She grinned that he would know her so well already. "That's exactly what I want. So what do you want?"

"What?"

"Well, if it *does* snow—which it won't, mind you—you need to pick something you would want so we can have an official bet." She bounced on her toes, raising her brows in anticipation. "So, Mr. Matthew Ellis, what is it that *you* want?"

"Something that *I* want?"

"Yes, and make it good so we're even. What is something that you *really* want?"

"Hmm…let's see." Matt's eyes danced with amusement as he pretended to think. After almost a minute, his expression grew serious, and he suddenly gazed at her as hot and hard as a branding iron. But before she could ask if something was wrong, he turned and swung open the truck door. "No bet."

"No bet? But why?"

"Because," he said quietly, "I just realized there's nothing you could possibly give me that I'd want." Then he climbed into his truck and slammed the door behind him.

• • •

Matt was strangely quiet after they left the winery, and Kennedy wondered what she did this time to set him off. It seemed she couldn't do anything right when she was around him. It'd be for the best for both of them if he just took her straight home.

"Are you hungry?" he asked, gazing straight ahead at the road.

"Not really." But as soon as her answer left her mouth, her belly betrayed her with a loud growl.

Stupid loud-mouthed stomach.

He glanced at her with a smirk. "Not hungry, huh?"

She flushed. "Okay, maybe I could eat something quick."

Matt put on his turn signal. "I know just the place. Afterward, I'll take you to the pier. There're some shops along the water you might like to go into."

He maneuvered through a few streets downtown and finally stopped at a restaurant called Tim and Kelly's. Once they walked in and were seated at a table, a pretty blond waitress came up to their table.

"Matt Ellis!" she exclaimed, planting a fist on her hip. "Boy, if seeing you isn't like getting an early Christmas present, I don't know what is. It's like you all but disappeared off the face of the earth."

Matt shifted uncomfortably but smiled back. "Hey, Brittany. I'm just here for lunch, but it's good to see you, too."

"Is it? Because you could have seen me a lot earlier if you'd called me back," she said, folding her arms.

Matt rubbed the back of his neck. "Yeah, uh, I haven't had a chance."

"Oh, really?"

"Things have been really hectic at the winery with the holidays and all."

Kennedy cleared her throat. When the waitress looked at her, she gave a little wave. "Hi. Don't mind me. Just wondering if I could get something to drink while you two finish your not-at-all-awkward discussion."

Brittany frowned. "Of course," she said, pulling out a pen and small tablet. "I know Matt will want his favorite beer that's on draft this week. What would you like?"

"Matt has great taste, so whatever he's having, I'll have."

"You might as well throw in a couple of orders of Tim's

special buffalo wings, too," Matt added.

"Great," Brittany said, sounding a hundred and eighty degrees from great. Then with a cold glance at Matt, she snapped her tablet closed and stalked off toward the bar.

Kennedy raised her brows at Matt. "Wow, at least our beers will be well chilled."

"Sorry about that. I kind of forgot Brittany worked here. We dated a few times."

"I gathered as much."

He blew out a long breath. "She's really a nice girl and all, but…"

"But she was looking for more of a commitment?"

Before Matt could answer, Brittany returned with their beers, promptly plopping them down in front of them. "Enjoy," she said with false sweetness.

After Brittany walked away, Kennedy took a tentative sip of her beer, half fearing the waitress might have poisoned her, but it was cold and citrusy and absolutely delicious.

Kennedy set her beer down and gave him a long look. "Are you really so opposed to having a relationship again? And if so, I can see why your mom is concerned."

"Yes, I'm really not interested. Been there. Done that. And my mom was born concerned. She worried about me even when I was engaged to Sam."

"Maybe she had a feeling Sam wasn't the right woman for you."

Matt picked up his beer and hesitated. "Yeah, maybe. Sam never really got along with my parents."

Kennedy almost choked. "What? How could she not get along with your mom? She's a total sweetheart."

He shrugged. "I don't know. It's not that they didn't get along. Sam wasn't exactly the domestic type, and I think that might have grated on my mom's nerves a bit and created tension. She feared our future children would starve to death before the age of two."

Brittany appeared again with a tray of chicken wings and set it on the center of the table, along with extra napkins and blue cheese sauce.

Matt took a wing and dug in.

"Did Sam get along with your sister?" she asked.

Matt sighed. "Enough questions about Sam." He dropped a chicken bone onto his plate then pointed at the tray. "You'd better eat while they're hot and there're still wings left," he said, picking up another one.

Matt was right. She didn't even know why she was so curious about his former fiancée anyway. Kennedy was starving, and the wings did look yummy. She took her fork and dug into a chicken wing, transferring it to her plate. She then picked up her knife and began to cut the meat off the bone.

Matt's face fell, and the wing he had between his fingers dropped to his plate with a *thunk*. "What the hell do you think you're doing?"

Kennedy finished chewing then swallowed. "Same as you. Eating chicken wings."

"No. *No*," he repeated, shaking his head. "Look, city girl, that is *not* how you eat chicken wings."

"Well, I'm doing it anyway." She stuck her fork into another piece of meat, placed it in her mouth, then smiled tightly for emphasis.

"I can't witness any more of this." Matt placed a hand over his eyes. "Stop right now. People know me here, for crying out loud."

"What in the world are you so worked up about?"

"The knife-and-fork thing. You do *not* eat chicken wings with a knife and fork. What, are you from France? You pick one up, like so," he said, taking one in between both his hands, "bring it to your mouth, and take a bite like every other red-blooded American."

She frowned. "I know that, but then I'll get sauce all over my fingers and face."

"Yes! Exactly. *Thank you*," he huffed, glancing at the ceiling.

She laughed at his horrified face as she continued to eat. And then laughed again when his expression turned annoyed from her laughing. Justin never got frustrated with her eating habits. But he was just as fastidious as she was. Hating the idea of getting all messy but not wanting to ruin their lunch over something so trivial, she calmly placed her silverware down and picked up a wing with her hands. "Better, Captain Caveman?"

"Much."

Hiding her amusement, she dunked her wing in blue cheese until it was coated. "You know, these are probably the best wings I've had in a long time. I never get to indulge in comfort food like this. Or at least, not very often. Justin prefers seafood or sushi. On special occasions, we'll grab some Italian in the North End. He's pretty health conscious these days."

Matt took a long swallow of his beer. "Well, you have to splurge around the holidays. It's in the state statutes."

"Thanks for helping me be such a law-abiding citizen, then."

"Anytime." The warmth of his smile echoed in his voice.

She smiled back and her heart thudded once, before returning to its normal rhythm.

She looked away. "So, uh, I read in your town newspaper that there's a Christmas parade this week. Santa will be in a lobster boat float. People are invited to bring their dogs in the parade as long as they're dressed in some sort of Christmas theme."

Matt nodded. "Unfortunately, yes, that is true."

"Why unfortunately?"

"My mother dragged us to that parade my whole childhood, as well as the tree lighting ceremony at City Hall and the gingerbread house competition. I think I'm a little over it."

"Well, it sounds like good clean family fun. I want to do all of it."

He wiped his hands with a Wet-Nap, looking amused. "And how old are you again?"

She made a face. "Do you think Caitlyn and your mom will take me?"

"Of course. They never miss it."

"Oh, that's wonderful."

Matt cocked his head, studying her. "You know, you surprise me, city girl. I can't believe you're really into that hokey small-town stuff."

Her cheeks grew warm under Matt's gaze, and she had to look away. "I know it must seem silly to you, but you don't understand. I never got to experience stuff like that when I was a kid. You know, the whole Norman Rockwell family experience. Those kinds of memories are priceless."

"Come on. Your upbringing couldn't have been all that bad."

She snorted. "It wasn't all that good, either."

"Tell me one good thing."

"What do you mean?"

"You have to have at least one good Christmas memory from your childhood. Tell me what it was."

One good memory? No one ever asked her that. Not even Justin.

She blinked at him then thought back. It didn't take her long. There was one time that stood out in her mind.

Kennedy settled back in her chair. "One Christmas Eve, when I was about ten, my mom and her husband—I call him Number Two—had to go to New York City for some business party."

"Wait. You call him Number Two because he was your mom's second husband?"

"Actually, no. I call him that because he was my mom's crappiest husband," she said with a smirk. "Anyway, Number Two didn't want me to come. He wanted to leave me home with a babysitter on Christmas Eve."

"That sucks."

She nodded. "Hence, his nickname. But my mom insisted I come with them. She bought me a really pretty dress and everything. So we all went to the party. It was okay. No other kids were there and the food wasn't what I liked, so I didn't eat. I could tell Number Two was just waiting for me to complain, so I didn't dare. Then, after a long while, my mom came over to me and whispered that she and I were going to sneak out of there for a bit. I was so excited. It was like our own little adventure. Just my mom and me. She took my hand, and we tiptoed out of the party as if we were fooling everyone. She hailed a cab, and it took us to the Little Italy. We stopped off at an Italian pastry shop and must have ordered at least six different desserts, where each one was better than the next. Even the hot chocolate was the best I ever had. And we just talked."

"Sounds nice."

"It was, but the best part was that my mom was happy. I didn't often see her that way, but on that particular day with just me and no one else around, she was truly happy. That was a good day." She blinked back a tear.

"That was a *very* good day," he said hoarsely. His gray eyes were gentle with understanding. Then without warning, he reached out his hand and gently stroked her cheek.

Her breath hitched as his touch sent tingles up her arm. She couldn't help herself and leaned in slightly at the comfort he offered. The warmth of his skin was intoxicating. Sort of like the man himself.

Little warning signals shot off in her head. *What are you doing? Abort! Abort!*

She jerked her head back.

Matt immediately dropped his arm. "Sorry," he blurted, looking just as shaken as she felt. "You, uh, had some wing sauce on your face." He quickly signaled the waitress for their check.

"Oh, right. Thanks." Shame filled her for enjoying his touch, but she sent him a tight smile then picked up her napkin and began to wipe where his fingers had just rested.

She had a feeling nothing was on her face. But she continued to scrub anyway, all too willing to play along with his lie and hope it was true. For both their sakes.

• • •

"Matt, are you sure you won't stay for dinner?" his mom asked.

He dug his hand into the bowl on his lap and shoved another fistful of popcorn into his mouth. "No, I'm good," he mumbled. "Thanks."

Stay for dinner? No friggin' way. He'd spent enough time with Kennedy today, between the winery, lunch, and then shopping along the pier. He didn't even know why he was still at the house. He should have left an hour ago. But then Caitlyn had come home from school begging him to help make popcorn garlands for the Christmas tree that they were supposed to pick out tomorrow night, and well, before he knew it he was pouring popcorn kernels into a pot.

But he'd be leaving soon. He'd better be leaving soon…

He cast a sidelong glance at Kennedy as he sorted the popcorn for them and shoved some more in his mouth. Kennedy laughed at something Caitlyn said as they compared their work. His sister had gotten creative and strung together cranberries she'd dipped in glue and glitter. Kennedy looked as if she was really enjoying his mom and sister's company.

Matt had sure enjoyed hers today. Perhaps a bit too much, which was starting to concern him. Kennedy had a sweet naïveté about her. He also liked her sense of humor, and although Kennedy's business was very important to her, she didn't seem the type to put her own ambition ahead of love. His ex Samantha could have taken some lessons from that concept. Not that it mattered anymore. He was over her, and over trying to find a woman to settle down with, but Kennedy was the type of woman who could get a guy thinking about it.

At this point, he just needed a little separation from her. Some breathing room so he could get his head on straight. Kennedy was going to be his sister-in-law soon. Thank God Justin was coming back tomorrow. Just in time. His mom wanted Matt to be nice to Kennedy, but any more time spent together, and he was afraid he'd take that to a whole other level.

"Matt, don't do that!"

"I didn't touch her!" he blurted, raising spread hands.

His mother snatched the bowl of popcorn from his lap. "What in the world are you talking about? I meant stop eating all the popcorn. We still need enough for ten more feet of garland."

"Oh, right. Sorry."

Kennedy laughed at him, an easy, soft sound. Her blue eyes were bright and shining behind those funky eyeglass frames of hers. She had a nice laugh. Kind of deep and throaty. Sexy.

Don't even go there, stupid. She's Justin's.

Matt rubbed the back of his neck. He needed to go home before he embarrassed himself further. But just as he stood up to say his good-byes, his cell phone went off. He glanced at it and saw it was none other than his brother. Perfect.

"Hey," Matt said, feeling guilty that his greeting lacked enthusiasm.

"Matt, I need you to do me a huge favor."

When did Justin *not* need him for a huge favor? But there was a desperate edge to his brother's tone, so Matt decided it might be more serious than he thought and sought some privacy in the kitchen. "What's the problem?" he asked, lowering his voice.

"I can't come home tomorrow."

Son of a— "Are you serious? Kennedy—not to mention Mom—is not going to be happy. What's the holdup this time?"

"Hear me out, bro. Things went really well today at the portfolio presentation. In fact, it went so well, they want my boss and me to have dinner and drinks with them tomorrow night at Morton's. Isn't that cool?"

"No. It's not cool. It's the holidays and you're supposed to be home for them—like the song indicates. With your fiancée," he added harshly.

Justin let out a long breath. "Look, it's just one more day. Then I promise I'll be home on the very next morning ferry."

"That's all well and good, but why are you telling me? Shouldn't you be explaining this to Kennedy?"

There was a pause. "That's where I need the favor."

Oh, hell to the no.

"Sorry, no can do, Justin. I draw the line at relationship interference."

"Oh, come on. I can't handle Kennedy getting all whiny on me. You know women better than any man."

Perhaps Matt did know women. He'd dated enough of them, which had to be the reason why he knew Kennedy wasn't a whiny kind of woman. But Justin should know that. Instead, it seemed as if his brother didn't know his own fiancée at all, which stirred his anger even more. Kennedy deserved better. She also deserved a freakin' engagement ring.

He had to remind himself it was none of his business.

"Please, Matt," his brother pleaded. "I wouldn't normally ask this, but I have another meeting in fifteen minutes. I don't want her feelings to get hurt, and I know I can trust you to explain it better than I ever could. So will you do this for me? For family."

Matt clenched his teeth. He was a moron and a complete sap, more so because he found himself agreeing. Anything to get off the phone before he told Justin off.

"Awesome. Thanks, man. It's nice to know I can always count on you."

"Yeah, yeah," Matt muttered. "Just get your ass on that ferry first thing Friday morning, okay?"

"Will do. See you then."

After Justin disconnected, Matt shoved his phone into his pocket and walked back into the living room.

His mom frowned when she saw his expression. "Who was that, dear? Is there a problem at the winery?"

Matt rubbed his forehead. "Uh, no. It was Justin."

Kennedy's gaze cut to him. Her eyes were wide and round as if offended Justin didn't call her first. Yeah, he didn't blame her one bit.

"Is he okay?" she asked.

For now, Matt thought bitterly. *Unless he pulls another stunt like this and puts that look on your face again. Then he's going to be toast.*

"What's the matter?" his mom asked.

"Um, nothing is the matter." He pasted on a smile he wasn't anywhere near feeling and went on. "In fact, everything is fantastic."

Flippin' freakin' fantastic.

Kennedy bit her lip. "Is it?"

"Oh, sure. It's just that Justin's portfolio thing went better than he hoped, and his boss wants to take him out to celebrate, since it's Christmas and everything. He won't be home until Friday now, but he promised something extra special for Kennedy when he comes home." *Or else…*

Kennedy's gaze fell to her lap. "He doesn't have to do that," she said quietly.

Kennedy's face, her obvious disappointment, was like a razor to his jugular. Slowly killing him. He had to stop the bleeding STAT. Then he quickly remembered what she'd told him at lunch. "Uh, the reason he called me was because he wanted to make sure I took Kennedy to Hospitality Night downtown for shopping, and then to the Christmas Tree lighting ceremony at city hall."

What the hell am I saying?

Caitlyn must have been wondering the same thing because she looked as if he'd grown an extra eyeball. "Matt, you hate that *quote* hokey *end quote* Christmas stuff. Last year when I asked you to take me, you said that you'd rather stick a—"

"You can come, too, Caitlyn."

His sister sat back with narrowed eyes. "Who are you and what have you done with my brother Matt?"

"You're a riot," he said with a deadpan look. "Did Mom enroll you in clown school on the side or something?"

She nudged Kennedy with her elbow. "Don't worry. We'll have a good time even *with* Matt there."

Kennedy's gaze traveled back to Matt. "Thanks. If it's not too much trouble, I'd love to go."

"Great." *AKA not great.* Because he was playing with fire here. The only saving grace he had was that there would be an eighteen-year-old smart-mouthed chaperone with them. *Thank you, God.*

As his sister drew Kennedy's attention back to her with a list of all the stores she had to see, his mother came over and patted him on the back. "I can't believe you'd do that for Justin. You're very sweet."

"That's what all the guys tell me down at the winery."

She chuckled, then, leaning in, added, "You *are* sweet. Especially because I know Kennedy's not your favorite person."

He glanced over at Kennedy's smiling face. He wanted to smile back, but guilt swooped in and punched him in the gut. "Yeah," he murmured, turning away, "it's a regular Christmas miracle."

. . .

True to his word, Matt did not stay for dinner. Thank goodness for small miracles. After the whole awkward lunch "incident," Kennedy felt a little space between them would be for the best. But his mom had received a phone call from her pharmacy telling her that her blood thinner was ready for pickup. Matt offered to get it for her and drop it by later that night. Kennedy hoped that meant *much* later.

After dinner, Kennedy and Caitlyn worked companionably side-by-side and helped clean up. She was feeling more and more a part of the family with each day. When all the dishes had been put away, Kennedy grabbed a pot off the stove and was about to place it in the sink, but she noticed it contained chopped fruit and smelled of cough medicine. "What's this?" she asked, wrinkling her nose.

Barbara smiled. "That's what we're baking with tonight."

Kennedy frowned into the pot of funky fruit again. There was definitely rum in it, but not a lick of chocolate anywhere. "Oh," she said, masking her disappointment, "I thought you said we'd be doing Christmas baking." *I.e. cookies. Chocolate cookies. Hint, hint.*

"Heavens, no," Barbara said with a chuckle. "I already

made cookies this afternoon while you were out."

Caitlyn hung up the dishtowel on the oven door. "That's right," she said with a smirk, "Mom likes to make them when no one is around so she can immediately hide them on us."

Barbara planted a hand on her hip. "I wouldn't need to hide them, missy, if you and Matt could control yourselves. If I left them out, there'd be none for Christmas."

Kennedy placed the pot back on the stove. "So what will we be making, then?"

"Tonight I'm going to show you how to make the famous Ellis fruitcake."

Fruitcake. Of all things. Her heart sank a little. "Oh… that…that sounds…" Unable to come up with a polite adjective, she let her sentence trail off.

Barbara nodded. "I know you'll love it. It was a particular favorite of my husband's, but the whole family looks forward to it every year. It's tradition. Isn't that right, Caitlyn?"

"That's right, Mom," she said brightly. "It wouldn't be Christmas without it."

Kennedy forced an enthusiastic smile, too. She could be into this as much as everyone else. After all, this was what she wanted: all the traditions that went with being a part of Justin's family. And she got it all right. Plus, the fruitcake.

She definitely got the fruitcake.

"I saved us a bit of time," Barbara added. "The chopped fruit and rum had to be boiled and then cooled for at least an hour, so I did that this afternoon, too. Why don't you sift the flour while I beat the butter?"

"And I'll supervise," Caitlyn offered with a laugh, flopping down on a stool behind them.

Her mom chuckled. "You mean wait to lick the bowl when we're done, don't you?" Barbara handed Kennedy the sifter and the bag of flour. "Honestly, the kids were like seagulls around the holidays whenever I was baking. Especially the boys. It seemed as if they had holes in their stomachs the way they ate. They all had major sweet tooths, that's for sure."

"Remember when Matt and Justin used to arm wrestle to see who'd get the first slice of fruitcake?" Caitlyn said, grinning.

"Oh, my, yes." She chuckled. "Dad would referee. For a while there, even that was becoming tradition, too. I know I have pictures of it in one of the albums. We can look through them later if you'd like."

"That would be wonderful." Kennedy had never seen any baby pictures of Justin and was even a bit curious to see what Matt had looked like as a little boy as well.

Barbara sighed happily as she beat the eggs. "Since Matt was the eldest, he realized the truth regarding Santa first, but he was so good about making sure Justin and Caitlyn still believed. He even took it upon himself to set his alarm clock to get up in the middle of the night and ring sleigh bells outside their bedroom doors."

Caitlyn's mouth dropped. "*Matt* was the one who did that? I had no idea. But man, when I was little he had me convinced that Santa had just come to our house."

"He was very protective of you two. Kind of like he is now, whether you want to believe it or not."

Kennedy smiled, enjoying hearing the kind of family life Justin had. And it made her all the more thankful that she would soon become a part of it. She also realized that she had misjudged Matt and how he'd first treated her. He truly had his brother's best interest at heart and was devoted to his family. It was one of the things she liked most about him. She handed Barbara the flour then went and brought the fruit mixture to her as well.

Barbara added all the ingredients together then transferred the mixture to a baking pan. "Believe it or not, this cake has to bake for two hours, then we lower the heat and bake it an additional thirty minutes. After it cools, we'll drizzle more rum on it." She elbowed Kennedy as she brought it to the oven. "The extra rum is what makes it extra good."

Kennedy and Caitlyn giggled as the back door flew open.

"Oh, I see how it is," Matt said, wiping his boots before entering the kitchen. "It's all fun and laughter when I'm not around."

Even in his mother's kitchen, Matt made a compelling presence, and suddenly Kennedy felt like a breathless girl of sixteen. She needed to get a grip.

"Yeah, it is more fun when you're not here," Caitlyn said with a teasing grin. "So thanks for bringing the party down with your arrival. We women were enjoying some quality bonding time."

Matt snorted. "Suddenly *you're* a woman?"

Caitlyn lifted her chin. "That's right. Kennedy even asked my advice on bridesmaid dresses."

He raised his hands mockingly. "Oh, well, then. I stand corrected."

Barbara took the prescription bag from his hand and kissed him on the cheek. "Thanks for picking up my medicine, dear."

"Not a problem." He arched an eyebrow at Kennedy. "So…bonding with the girls, huh?"

"And making fruitcake," his mother added in a singsong voice.

Matt exchanged amused glances with Caitlyn. "Ah, yes. Wouldn't be Christmas without the fruitcake."

Kennedy narrowed her eyes. *Hmm… Something definitely fruity is going on here.*

"Ha, see?" his mom exclaimed, turning to Kennedy. "Caitlyn said the exact same thing. I told you they look forward to it every year."

Suddenly the phone rang. Barbara glanced at the clock

on the microwave and frowned. "Oh, dear. That has to be my church group calling again. This is the first year I'm not helping with the Senior Christmas Dinner, and it's been chaos. I'd better get that," she said, rushing into the living room.

Kennedy folded her arms, determined to be let in on the joke. "You know what's fascinating?" she asked, taking a step closer to Matt. "It isn't very often that one finds a whole entire family completely crazy about fruitcake."

Matt didn't meet her gaze. "Yeah, I guess that is kind of interesting."

"It's ridiculous," she said, throwing her hands up. "And totally defies odds because less than two percent of people like fruitcake. So, listen, buddy, if I'm going to be a part of this family, I want the truth." She poked him in the chest to make sure he knew she meant business.

Matt looked at his sister. "What do you think?"

"We can let her in on the secret," Caitlyn said with a huge grin. "She's definitely one of us."

Matt hesitated. "Okay. The truth is…we all hate the fruitcake."

"I knew it!" she exclaimed then frowned. "But I don't understand. Why pretend to like it, then?"

"Honestly? Because none of us has the heart to tell her the truth. It makes her so happy. She's one of the two percent who actually enjoys it."

"And your dad," she added. "He liked it, too. Your mom said so."

Matt shook his head gravely. "No, he hated it the most."

Kennedy blinked then looked to Caitlyn. "He did?"

"Yup." Caitlyn shrugged. "Like Matt said, we didn't have the heart to make her feel bad on Christmas. At least this time she didn't put any figs or dried pineapple in it. That was a particularly bad year. Although Justin tolerated it the best out of all of us."

Kennedy cracked a smile. "So your mom goes through all this trouble of making a fruitcake every Christmas and she's the only one who eats it?"

"Oh, no," Matt assured her. "We'll all choke down a slice. You, too, since you'll soon be part of the family. And we'll all tell her how great it is. It's tradition."

"Tradition," Caitlyn echoed firmly.

Kennedy laughed. Oh my, if she didn't already love this family, this aspect of it only endeared them to her more. "Well, your secret is safe with me. I love traditions myself."

"That's good," Caitlyn said, cracking herself up, "because you and Matt are standing under the mistletoe."

What?!

Kennedy cautiously looked up as if to find the Sword of Damocles dangling over her, but instead found a small green ball of mistletoe tied up with ribbon. Crap! Her gaze dropped to Matt, who held a gleam of interest in his eyes, and her cheeks caught fire.

"Oh, well, that's a silly tradition," she said hurriedly, "I mean, we don't have to do that." *Do we?*

Barbara walked back into the room. "What don't you have to do?"

Caitlyn pointed to the ball. "Matt and Kennedy are under the mistletoe."

"Oh, how nice," Barbara said, clasping her hands. "Kiss her, Matt. It's Christmas after all."

Matt glanced at Kennedy and stiffened, but without further argument leaned in to her. Her heart fluttered like a hummingbird in anticipation. She caught the pleasant scent of pine and soap on his skin as he brushed his lips against her cheek, hovering for just a few brief seconds before he was once again at a safe distance from her. Such a simple kiss, yet her emotions whirled and skidded.

"I'd better get going," Matt murmured, backing into the

door.

His mom frowned. "Are you okay, dear? Maybe you should sit down a bit first."

"No, I need to get kissing—er, going. I need to *go*." His gaze reluctantly returned to hers, and his voice dipped. "I'll see you tomorrow night?"

She nodded, not trusting her voice. Then he was out the door as if suddenly spooked.

Unfortunately, she knew exactly how he felt.

Chapter Seven

Kennedy finished the last of the software proposals she'd been working on for a few new investors, then decided to let it sit for a day before sending them out. Everything was riding on them, so she had to make sure it was done right—and it would be. She couldn't tolerate anything less. Order and control came second only to air and water for her.

She scrolled through her emails for the third time that morning. Normally, she'd get anywhere from 50-100 emails a day. For some reason it looked a little light. Not even any joke emails from her cousin.

Relax, Kennedy. People know you're away, and they don't want to bother you.

Holiday breaks were going on. Family time. It had nothing whatsoever to do with people taking their business someplace else. After all, per *Boston* magazine, she was the matchmaking queen of the Back Bay. *For now, anyway.* Control slipping, she eyed the paper bag she had next to her.

Stupid stress-induced asthma. She picked it up and took a slow, measured breath. Everything would be fine. It had taken years to build her business. Surely it couldn't be destroyed in a matter of one Christmas vacation.

Maybe she'd put a call in to Mia. Just a brief check-in. Nobody could fault her for that. She and Justin were both workaholics. It was what drew them together in the first place. They understood perfectly how each other's minds worked. But even with all that, as much as she empathized with Justin working a few extra days on their vacation, a part of her still felt neglected. Hurt that she wouldn't come first in his life just once. Especially at Christmas.

Who was she kidding? Even *her* first thought had been to call Mia, and not her fiancé. Work came first for her, too. She and Justin really were two peas in a pod.

She picked up her cell phone. After two rings, Mia answered. "Match Made Easy, this is Mia Reynolds. Let's make your match today."

Kennedy smiled into her phone. "Is that greeting something new you're trying out while I'm away?"

"Kennedy! You're not supposed to be calling now. You're supposed to be enjoying the holidays with Justin."

Thankful that Mia couldn't see her face, she said, "Oh, we're not doing anything special right now." *Or anything at all.* "Since I had a free moment, I thought I'd see how you were holding up. "

"Well, okay then. Since you asked… I ended up hiring that escort we both liked. He'll be a great addition. Handsome and dependable. I also have a meeting with Celeste, the new marketing consultant, tomorrow."

She jerked to her feet. "You're meeting without me?"

"Tomorrow was the only time we could do it before Christmas." Mia paused. "Is that a problem?"

Is it? "Uh, no, no. Not at all." It wasn't like she had to control every aspect of Match Made Easy. That's why she had Mia as her right-hand woman in the first place, so she wouldn't have to be overseeing things 24/7. But still, a part of her felt queasy in loosening the reins.

Mia let out a relieved-sounding breath. "Great. Oh, and I had an email from someone who saw your presentation in Vegas. He wants to talk with you about the matchmaking software. I set up a meeting with him for the day you come back."

"That's perfect." She bit her lip, almost afraid to ask the next question. "So, did you happen to run the test group on the software yet?"

"I did!" she gushed. The phone dropped, and she heard papers being shuffled. "Okay, I have the results right here. We had nineteen out of twenty successful love matches. And the only reason we didn't get twenty out of twenty was because one of the couples had to postpone their date for a death in the family."

"Awesome! Er, not about the death in the family. About the success rate. Wow, I can't believe it."

"You should be the last person who's surprised," Mia said with a laugh. "Look at you and Justin. That couldn't have been a fluke. You guys obviously only have eyes for each other."

Kennedy swallowed, her throat feeling tight. "Yeah… eyes for each other," she murmured.

Right? She *did* only have eyes for Justin. He was everything she wanted in a husband. It was just…while she may have had eyes for Justin, sometimes her *thoughts* wandered to Matt and those shoulders of his that could hold a family of four. She'd had such a fun time with him the other day when he'd taken her to the winery and to lunch. Matt was a surprisingly good listener, too. She shared things with him that she hadn't even shared with Justin. It was that easy. The way he looked at her with those beautiful, intense gray eyes made her feel like what she had to tell him was the most interesting thing in the world.

Ugh. Beautiful eyes. She was behaving just like her

mother. Allowing her hormones to overrule good, logical common sense. Kennedy was afraid the apple didn't fall far from *that* tree. She was throwing a monkey wrench into everything because her feelings were all over the place. She needed to gain some control. Like Mia had said, her matchmaking software was a success. She had to remember that. More importantly, she needed to stick to the match that was designed so perfectly for her.

Mia cleared her throat. "One other thing, I noticed our competition is doing TV commercials and some other heavy advertising. Do you think we should look into something like that, too?"

Kennedy bit her lip until it throbbed like a pulse. Television commercials were expensive. However, if that was their next step to stay competitive, then she couldn't rule it out. "You know what, why don't you run it by Celeste and get her take. Maybe she'll want to start in February, closer to rollout. Whatever she feels is best, I'll be onboard with."

"Okay, great. And don't worry, Kennedy. Nobody in the office is worried about the business. We totally believe in your work and are behind you one hundred percent."

Well, it was nice to know somebody believed in her— even if she didn't quite believe in herself. Her employees were so loyal. Unfortunately, the stress of carrying that knowledge was doing a number on her mental state, not to mention breathing state. She fingered the paper bag again.

"Kennedy, are you still there?"

"Oh, uh, yes," she wheezed. "Thanks for the update."

"Anytime, boss. Oh, and Kennedy?"

She rubbed her forehead, feeling a monster of a headache looming. "Yes?" she asked wearily.

"Have a Merry Christmas."

Yeah, good luck with that one. "Merry Christmas to you, too."

Kennedy ended the call and tossed her phone on the bed. Some Christmas. Her fiancé was in Boston, her business was in limbo, and she, despite her own excellent matchmaking abilities, was suddenly drawn to her future brother-in-law.

She was completely losing it.

Santa, I hope you're real because I have a whopper of a Christmas list in the making…

There was a knock on her bedroom door. *What now?* She closed her laptop and brushed her paperwork aside. "Come in," she called.

Caitlyn walked in wearing a sweater with a giant snowman on the front. Her long blond hair was pulled into a ponytail, showcasing candy cane earrings. "Hey, Kennedy. I just got home, since I had a half day at school. I'm officially on winter break now. Woo-woo," she said with a fist pump.

Kennedy laughed. "That's great."

Caitlyn sat on her bed. "I was kind of thinking that maybe you and I could do something this afternoon. Just us. You know, before Matt takes us downtown."

Matt. Right. He was supposed to bring them Christmas shopping tonight. She should call Justin. If anything, to hear his voice. Remind her of who she loved and was pledged to — and more importantly, who she should be thinking about.

She swallowed. "I'd like that. What did you have in mind?"

Caitlyn wiggled her fingers. "Manicures?"

Kennedy smiled. She glanced at her hands and figured her nails could use a little up keeping. "Perfect."

"Great." Caitlyn made herself more comfortable, drawing her legs up, hugging her knees to her. "So, you don't have any brothers or sisters?"

"No, I don't." She sighed, then gave a resigned shrug. "My cousin, Trent, is the closest thing I have to a brother." He was the one constant in her life. The one who kept in touch with her when her mom would remarry, and they would ship off to another location like nomads. It was such a time of disarray. Of people quickly coming into her life and then leaving just as fast. Chaos. The last time her mom married, Kennedy hadn't even bothered unpacking. Decided to just live out of her suitcases. Her stepfather thought she had a rebellious streak. She called it being practical.

They divorced six months later.

Caitlyn placed a small hand on her arm. "We're your family now."

"Thank you," she said, touched at the sincerity in her voice.

"It's going to be so great when you finally marry Justin. Can I be a bridesmaid?"

She nodded. "Absolutely."

"Awesome. I always wanted to be in a wedding." Caitlyn swung her legs down and stood. "I'll let my mom know we'll be leaving soon. And I'll text Matt and tell him to pick us up at five. That'll give us plenty of time to get our nails done, and then afterwards we can all grab dinner downtown together. You have to try PJ's. They have the best burgers. Tonight is going to be so much fun," she said, skipping to the door. "Funny, but I think of you like a sister already."

Kennedy couldn't help but smile. "I feel the same."

Caitlyn left then popped her head back in the room. "Oh, and I know Matt thinks of you like a sister, too," she added before disappearing again.

Kennedy's shoulders slumped. With regards to Matt, she *wished* she felt the same.

• • •

After stuffing her face with the best hamburger she'd ever had, Kennedy popped into a few stores on the downtown avenue to do a little Christmas shopping of her own. She bought Barbara some fancy soaps and shower gels and picked up a cute pink sweater for Caitlyn. When Caitlyn and Matt went for coffee, she even managed to find a gift for Matt: a leather wine journal. She thought he might like something to organize his tasting notes. She already had in her mind that she would put the first entry in for him and mark down the pinot noir they'd tasted together that day he gave her a tour of the winery.

It was the very least she could do for him. After all, Matt had given her a gift that day when he had asked her to recall a favorite childhood memory. She hadn't thought back on that Christmas Eve in ages, and she was glad she had. She'd always cherish that reminder of her mom. Matt was becoming quite special to her—as any future brother-in-law would, she told herself—and she wanted to make the most of her time with Justin's family. Create some lasting Christmas memories.

That's all she'd have soon enough. Memories. After all, after New Year's, she and Justin would head back to Boston. She probably wouldn't see Matt and the family until closer to the wedding—whenever that would be. They'd had to change the date twice because of each other's work conflicts. And if they couldn't nail down a date to get married, the chance of making it back to Cape Fin for regular visits seemed virtually impossible. A fresh pain squeezed in her heart at the thought. She already was missing them.

Kennedy adjusted the bags she had in her grip and walked along the sidewalk. The air was cold but still, and she was enjoying just watching the crowds, soaking up the festive atmosphere. Horse-drawn carriage rides were being offered up and down the main street, and parents and children lined up at city hall to take pictures outside with Santa in a lifeguard boat.

"Kennedy, there you are!" She turned the corner, and Caitlyn came running up to her.

Matt approached her at a more leisurely pace, carrying a

paper cup in his right hand. "We were worried you got lost. Caitlyn thought you might be cold and need something to warm you up," he said, handing her the cup.

Caitlyn frowned. "No, I didn't. It was Matt's idea. He said you love hot chocolate."

Kennedy raised her eyebrows at him. "How do you know I love hot chocolate? Did Justin tell you?" She took the lid off and smiled when she saw there was whipped cream and sprinkles on top.

Matt shrugged. "I just noticed you drinking the stuff at the house a lot. That's all."

"The *stuff*?" She raised an eyebrow at him. "So I suppose you never drink hot chocolate?"

"Nope." He thumped his chest with his fists. "I drink more manly drinks."

Caitlyn rolled her eyes. "Right. Matt the manly man here had an extra-large hot chocolate with two chocolate-dipped candy canes in it."

Matt grabbed his sister by the waist and rubbed his knuckles over her head. "Quiet, you. You're ruining my rep."

Kennedy laughed. "Don't worry, I don't think any less of you."

"Which means she doesn't think any *more* of you either," Caitlyn quipped, jumping out of Matt's arms.

"Okay, you two have had your fun. At my expense," he added dryly. He checked his watch. "We should head over to get a Christmas tree now before all the good ones are gone."

"Let's surprise Mom with a huge one this year. Like, twelve feet tall," Caitlyn said, raising her hand way over her head for emphasis.

"A twelve-foot tree?" Matt took the bags from Kennedy's hands then led them both back to the car. "Yeah, that'll be a surprise all right, ding dong, considering the house has ten-foot ceilings."

Caitlyn pursed her lips. "Well, we need an extra special tree, since Justin and Kennedy are here."

"Oh, you guys don't have to go to so much trouble for us. I usually get a little four-foot tree for my condo, and Justin doesn't put up any tree. Just as long as we decorate it all together when Justin makes it back, I'll be happy."

"*If* Justin makes it back to decorate," Matt mumbled.

Kennedy bristled. "He *will* make it back."

"We'll see."

What is that supposed to mean? "Oh yeah, well, when I spoke with him this morning, he couldn't wait to come back. He said he loves me and misses me terribly." She didn't know why she was getting all defensive or why she had to emphasize how much Justin loved her. But Matt implying that his brother would somehow come up with another excuse to stay in Boston rubbed her the wrong way—probably because the same notion had crossed her own mind as well. But Justin had promised her, which was why she'd accepted his proposal in the first place. He'd promised her to be more attentive to spending time with her versus time at the office. She'd agreed to be mindful of it as well. The week was still young, so she was still willing to give Justin the benefit of the doubt.

Once they came up to the car, Matt threw Kennedy's bags inside and slammed the door. "They sell the Christmas trees at the end of the street," he said gruffly. "We can walk."

Not trusting her voice, since she was still miffed at Matt, she gave a short nod.

They only made it one block when Caitlyn pointed. "There's Lane and Ava. I'm going to go say hi to them. Catch up with you guys in a bit, okay?"

Obviously Caitlyn wasn't really asking for permission, because she darted off before either of them even digested what she'd said. She and Matt were left alone in awkward silence. She shot him a cold look before turning her nose up and continuing the rest of the way ahead of him.

They came upon the Christmas tree nursery set-up and entered through its decorated gates. Christmas trees of all shapes and varieties were lined up in even rows. Colored lights were strung along the fence and "The Christmas Song" by Nat King Cole blared in the background as they made their way down the paths, dodging other tree shoppers in the process.

"Hey, sorry about what I said about Justin not making it back," he offered, coming up alongside her.

She glanced at him. He seemed sincere, so she relented a little. "It's okay."

"No, it's not. I was being a jerk."

You can say that again. But she supposed she wasn't an angel, either. It seemed as if they brought out the worst in each other. She turned and gave him a slight smile. "I can't really blame you. You've had to step in and be a kind of replacement for Justin to me. You, uh, must be pretty tired of that."

"I'm not tired of it."

She stopped walking. "You're not?"

He stopped, too, his gray eyes drinking her up. "No, I'm not." His gaze dropped and froze on her lips. Just as her stomach was about to take a tiny dip, he turned away and pointed at the tree in front of them. "What do you think of this one?"

She blinked then glanced at the tree. She had to admit it was very pretty. The coloring was bluish green, and it had an almost perfect triangular shape. "I love it. Let's buy it."

"Let's buy it? Woman, have you ever picked out a live Christmas tree before?"

With some embarrassment, she shook her head.

"Okay, then. Here's your first lesson. We check the soil," he said, squatting down. She remained standing. Matt felt the soil with his fingertips, much like she imagined he'd do in his vineyard. "Soft and moist is a good sign."

"If you say so."

He grinned up at her. "Don't like to get your hands dirty?"

She hesitated. "Don't be ridiculous."

His eyes narrowed. "Oh, yeah? Then come down here and check it with me."

Righto. She could do that. It was just dirt. What was the big deal? She slowly bent down next to him.

Matt took hold of her hand as if he didn't trust her to do it herself and slowly slipped her glove off. "Stick your hand in the soil," he told her.

"Why? You just told me the soil was perfect."

He cocked his head at her. There was a gleam in his eyes as if he discovered something hilarious but wanted to keep it a secret. "Maybe you should double-check me."

"I trust you." She tried to pull her hand away.

"Aw, come on," he cajoled. "A little dirt never hurt anyone."

She huffed out a breath. "Fine!" She dug her fingers into the soil. *Eww.* Just as he told her, the soil was wet and a bit muddy. "Happy?"

"Kind of," he said, grinning. "Now check the firmness of the root ball."

Closing her eyes, she prayed for serenity. "Tell me you didn't just suggest that."

He chuckled. "It's important that the root ball that's bound in that burlap is firm. If it's not, there's probably a good chance that the tree won't survive."

She poked at the root. "Solid as a cantaloupe."

Matt nodded. He then took her hand and pulled her up, letting his fingers linger a moment too long in its hold. She inhaled sharply at the contact. "Run your hand along the branches," he suggested. "We want green needles, but also we don't want to lose too many of them when we do that."

With her already dirty hand, she checked the branches

with him. "Honestly, Matt, if you tell me you've changed your mind about this tree after all this, I'm going to clobber you."

He laughed. "No, this tree is the one. It'll look great in my mom's house, too."

"Thank goodness." Her fingers were covered in soil and dirt. Normally she carried hand sanitizer with her, but she'd thrown her handbag in the car when they'd stopped to drop off her packages. She tried to shake some of it off but her hand was still a mess. *Matt is so going to pay for this.* She strategically held her arm away from her body so she wouldn't get anything on her coat.

Matt rolled his eyes then took her arm and began wiping her hand with a handkerchief he'd pulled from his coat pocket. "You don't like to get messy, do you, city girl?"

"Well, what kind of question is that? Who likes to get dirty? And stop calling me 'city girl.'" She tried to pull her hand back but he held on tightly. His grip was strong, firm… protective. It caused disturbing quakes to her serenity.

"I didn't say anything about dirt. I said you don't like messes."

She stiffened. No, she did not like messes. She preferred neat and tidy. Orderly. It probably stemmed from the whole control problem she had going. Probably because she had so little control growing up. It was one of the reasons she was drawn to Justin. He was just as much of a control freak as she was. But he also made her feel secure and steady. Unlike Matt, who had a way of making her feel unbalanced and out of control.

She lifted her chin. "So what? Are you making fun of me because of that?"

He dropped her hand and gave her a long look. "Not at all. But it must be exhausting to be so perfect all the time."

"What's wrong with perfect?"

"Perfect is boring, you know? In my opinion, everybody

needs a little mess now and then."

"I'm sure you've had plenty of messes in your life," she retorted. "Maybe *you* could use perfection and a little stability now."

His gaze met hers. "Maybe."

He was doing it again. Studying her with a curious intensity and creating that unbalanced feeling she hated. Her mind was swimming in a haze of feelings and desires. It took her almost a full minute to even notice that it had begun to snow.

Caitlyn came rushing over to them. "Hey, did you guys find a tree yet?"

Matt nodded. "Yeah, this one. What do you think?"

His sister's face lit up. "It's perfect. Wait until Mom and Justin see it. Can you believe it's snowing? Lane said he heard the weather channel predicting huge accumulations overnight. We're in for a white Christmas after all," she said happily.

Kennedy looked at Matt. "Good thing we didn't make that bet about the weather," she said, brushing the cold powder off her coat. "I would've had to pay you in full."

"Gut feeling trumps technology once again."

"Oh, please. You got lucky."

"No, but I think you really did."

"What do you mean?"

"Wasn't it technology that brought you and Justin together?"

She didn't like where this was going. "Yes, but—"

"Nice and controlled. Easy. No mess," he added in a gruff whisper. "A regular match made in heaven."

"Or a regular *match made easy* in heaven," Caitlyn said with a giggle. "See what I did there?"

"Yeah. Cute." Kennedy pasted on a smile, but it felt brittle on her lips. Because as she watched Matt turn and walk away, she couldn't help but feel that her engagement to Justin was becoming anything *but* easy.

Chapter Eight

The next morning Kennedy woke up and saw snow falling. She hopped out of bed and looked more closely out the window. *Crikey.* It must have snowed all night because it looked to be at least a foot of accumulation so far.

How can that be? She had seen the forecast before they'd left town. Not that she was against having a white Christmas, but none of the weathermen had mentioned anything about potential blizzard conditions.

A knock sounded on her bedroom door. Combing her hair with her fingers, she walked over to open it. Mrs. Ellis stood there wearing a look of concern in her eyes.

"Good morning, Barbara. Are you okay?" she asked.

Barbara smiled but wrung her hands. "Good morning, dear. I'm fine, just worried about Justin. He's not answering his cell phone. Have you talked to him yet this morning?"

Considering that it was before office hours and how often he had his cell phone glued to his hand, she found it a bit concerning, too. But there had to be a logical explanation. "Uh, no, not yet, but maybe he's in the shower."

His mom's face visibly relaxed. "You're right. I'm getting paranoid. It's just that the weather is pretty bad, and they're thinking it's going to continue all day. They shut down all the ferries until visibility is better."

"There's no ferry service?" She paused, her thoughts swimming. But that meant…

Barbara reached out and laid a hand on her arm. "Justin can't come home today," she said, mimicking Kennedy's thoughts.

Seriously?! Kennedy raised a hand to her head, feeling slightly lightheaded. So much for their special time together. Their holiday vacation was becoming a joke.

"I'm sure they'll be running by tomorrow."

Tomorrow? She needed to sit before she fainted.

"Don't worry, dear. Matt will come by soon. He'll build us a nice fire, and we'll decorate the tree. Doesn't that sound like fun?"

"Um…"

More time with Matt? Ohmygosh, no. That sounded completely and utterly horrendous. She needed time *away* from him. Time so she could forget how he could make her heart jolt with one steamy look. Time so she could forget how he could make her laugh. Time so she could remember all the reasons why he was so wrong for her—especially the most important one being that he was her *fiancé's brother.* "I need to call Justin," she blurted.

His mom raised her eyebrows at her outburst. "Of course you do. I'll let you do that. Tell him I love him and to be careful driving. In the meantime, I'll go make some coffee and some cranberry muffins. Come downstairs whenever you're ready."

She managed a weak smile. "Thanks, Barbara."

As soon as his mom left, she closed the door and made a beeline for her phone. She had to hear Justin's voice again, something to give her the reassurance she needed. She pressed "send" and waited. After three rings, it went straight to voicemail.

With slumped shoulders, she sat. Justin would call her today when he had a free moment. He would. However, knowing that didn't help her right now. She needed a moment to reorient herself before she saw Matt and the rest of the family.

Then she knew what she had to do. She hit a new number and then "send" again.

This time a male voice answered before the second ring. "Hey, Kennedy," her cousin said.

"Put Maddie on," she barked into the phone.

"Now, what the hell kind of hello is that?" Trent asked.

Kennedy rolled her eyes. "*Hello*, Trent. Now, please put Maddie on the phone. It's kind of an emergency."

"Emergency? But I'm your cousin," he said, sounding petulant. "Why are you asking for my fiancée? She may not even be around."

Jeez, and people say women are the dramatic ones. "Look, Trent, I love you. You know that. But right now I need some… *womanly* advice."

"She's right here."

Kennedy heard whispering between the two, then Maddie's voice came on the line sounding tentative. "Hello?"

"Maddie, hi. It's me, Kennedy."

"Hi, um, what's going on? Trent said something about a womanly emergency."

"Yeah. Sort of."

"Are you pregnant?" she whispered.

"Goodness NO!" Ha! She'd actually have to be in the same town with her fiancé for *that* to happen.

"Well, what's up then?"

"Oh, you know, just…" *Snowed in on a small island while having the hots for my future brother-in-law.* She cleared her throat. "Not much."

Maddie chuckled. "Kennedy, it's nine o'clock in the morning, and you're supposed to be enjoying your time off with your fiancé, but instead you're calling here telling your cousin there's an emergency. Is everything okay?"

She bit her lip. *Depends on what your definition of okay is.* "I, um, I think I'm having a nervous breakdown."

"*What?* Why do you think that?"

"I'm screwing up my life, and I don't know how to stop it. Everything is going wrong." Then to her horror, she burst into tears.

"Oh, honey, don't cry!" Maddie sounded frantic. "Listen to me, you're not screwing up your life. You are running a very successful matchmaking company—one I happen to be very partial toward since I wouldn't be getting married without it. And not only that, you have a wonderful and handsome fiancé yourself. And it's Christmas time. Those all sound like wonderful things to me. Now tell ole Maddie how you could be ruining any of that?"

Kennedy sniffed. "I…" She sniffed again. "I think I'm developing feelings for Justin's brother." She held her breath and waited.

Maddie let several seconds go by before responding. "Well, what *kind* of feelings?" she asked.

"The NC-17 kind."

"Oh dear."

She hung her head. "I know! It's so wrong. This shouldn't happen. My computer matching program has a ninety-nine percent accuracy rating. It *can't* happen." It absolutely couldn't. She had investors who specifically signed on because of her relationship with Justin as proof of how well the software worked. She was counting on that money to pay for the advertising start-up costs.

"Maddie, I'm supposed to have those thoughts about

Justin. And now I'm not only confused, but I'm also feeling tremendously guilty, too. And I can't breathe," she said, clutching her chest.

"Oh dear."

"Let me grab my paper bag." Kennedy put down the phone and raised the bag to her lips. After several slow, deep breaths, she felt marginally better. She picked up the phone again. "Okay, I'm back."

"Does Justin know about these…feelings for Matt?"

"Oh, gosh, no! But honestly, how can he? He was called back into work and hasn't been around at all this past week."

"Oh dear."

"Stop saying that!"

"Sorry! Okay, let's think about this rationally for a second. You might be panicking for no reason."

She straightened and wiped her eyes. "Really?"

"Why sure, honey. Look, it's the holidays, and you've taken time away from work, which is very stressful. Plus, this is the first time you haven't been with your family for Christmas. Then Justin leaves you unexpectedly all alone. Naturally you're going to be drawn to any kind of attention shown to you."

Kennedy thought about that for a minute. Her mood lifted a fraction of an inch. "Matt *has* been showing me a lot of attention lately, but only because he's been kind of a stand-in for Justin."

"Think about this. How does Justin make you feel when you're with him?"

She thought back and pictured Justin's boyish, smiling face. "Calm. Secure. Loved."

"Exactly. And how does Matt make you feel?"

Matt's intense, sexy gaze popped into her mind and she frowned. "Out of control. Unstable. Wanted."

"*Okaaay.* I can see why you're confused. But trust me.

Those feelings you're having are just due to the situation, which is only temporary."

"Yeah. Only temporary. That makes total sense. Plus, Matt told me he isn't interested in marriage at all. He was engaged once, and I think that kind of scarred him."

"Well, there ya go. You're obviously all wrong for one another, and I'm not even a matchmaker," she said, chuckling.

Kennedy's lips twitched. "No, but if you ever need a job, I'll hire you. Thanks for talking me through this crisis."

"Anytime, honey. You'll be fine once you see Justin again. Then you'll forget all about Matt. I'll see you after the holidays."

Kennedy hung up feeling a thousand times better. Somehow, Maddie managed to put everything into perspective for her. These thoughts she'd been having about Matt were just a phase because Matt was here and Justin wasn't. Of course! She loved Justin. She would never ever betray him. And as soon as he returned and they could spend Christmas together, she'd realize even more how perfectly matched they really were.

• • •

Matt came in through the front door and shook the snow off his boots.

"Oh, Matthew," his mom said, "thank heavens. You've been out there shoveling forever."

Matt grunted in response. He hadn't been sleeping well. He could think of little else besides Kennedy lately. And now this friggin' snow storm had delayed his brother's return yet again. It also gave Matt the crazy urge to truck through the snow this morning and make sure in person that Kennedy and his family hadn't lost power and were taken care of.

"I was worried you were going to get frostbite," his mom

went on.

He took off his coat and looked up. His mom was with Caitlyn and Kennedy, sitting in front of the fire with boxes of Christmas ornaments around them. The three of them looked as if they were in the middle of a Christmas card photo shoot. "I'm okay. Just need to warm up inside a bit."

"Well, you're not going back out in this weather tonight. I already made Justin's room up for you, since Kennedy is staying in your old one."

"Mom, I—"

"No, excuses," she said in her *I-mean-business* mom voice. "It's too dangerous. Now why don't you come over here and help us decorate the tree."

"Yes, Ma'am." He chuckled then inadvertently glanced at Kennedy. She had on a red sweater that brought out the fire in her long red hair. She wore matching eyeglass frames again, something he found a little quirky yet endearing about her. Her slender fingers were working on unwrapping some tinsel that had gotten tangled on one of the ornaments. He also happened to note that she had yet to look up since he came in.

He wondered if she was still upset with him for what he'd said about her computer program last night. It was jealousy toward his brother that had him throwing out those nasty remarks. Sometimes his mouth just had a mind of its own. But he couldn't help it. He knew exactly what he'd seen: the rush of pink on her cheeks whenever their gazes met and the way her hands trembled when he took them in his own. She was attracted to him. Just as much as he was attracted to her. Thank goodness neither of them had the guts to say or do anything about it.

He walked over to her, his movements stiff and awkward as if his body knew better than his head to stay clear of her. But he couldn't help himself. "Just how many pairs of eyeglasses do you own?" he asked her.

"Ten," she answered, still keeping her gaze focused on her task at hand.

He stuck out his hands to the fire to warm them up. "A pair to match every outfit, huh?"

His sister huffed out a breath. "Oh, leave Kennedy alone, Matt. At least *she* has style."

"What, and I don't?" He spread out his arms and slowly turned around. "I'll have you know this is the best piece of flannel I own."

Caitlyn snorted. "Now I know what I'm getting you for Christmas."

"Yeah, yeah. And I know what I'm getting *you* for Christmas. I just need to pick a color. The vet's still sizing the muzzle."

Caitlyn stuck her tongue out at him but grinned.

He snuck another glance at Kennedy, who was ignoring the conversation as she placed ornaments on the tree. For some reason she seemed quiet and out of sorts today. Maybe it had to do with Justin. Hearing that your fiancé was going to be delayed again in making it back onto the island would step on anyone's Christmas spirit.

Matt reached into one of the boxes and pulled out a Snoopy ornament. An old favorite. His parents had bought that for him when he was seven. It reminded him of the Snoopy pajamas he'd seen Kennedy wear, and it brought a smile to his lips. Looked as if they had more in common than they originally thought. After placing a hook on it, he walked over to Kennedy's side of the tree and hung it. She smelled incredible—floral and fresh—and he had sudden regrets about moving closer to her. He took a step back then surveyed her work.

"Your ornament hanging is very...symmetrical," he commented.

Still kneeling, she looked at where he was staring and tilted her head. "What's wrong with that?"

"Nothing." He shrugged. "If you like perfectly symmetrical trees that is."

"I take it you do not."

The devil in him made him grin. She was just too easy to tease. "That's right. I do not."

"Well." She huffed. "Good thing *you're* not marrying me, then."

"Yeah. Good thing." *Very good thing.* Like the two of them could ever be together. He didn't even want a wife. And she belonged to his brother...

And that was a certain weird, wrong line you never crossed. Ever.

"Okay, enough, you two," his mom said, chuckling.

Kennedy stood up and bumped into him. "Oh, sorry," she said, trying to maneuver around him. But when she went one direction, he went in the same. She laughed, and that familiar shiver of awareness went through him as he breathed in her scent.

She was driving him crazy.

"My fault." He reached out and held her in place as he skirted around her. Unfortunately, touching her was his second mistake, and the tingling in his hands proved it. Stupid attraction. Why couldn't Justin have brought home one of the self-absorbed models he used to be so found of? But no, he had to go and bring home an anal retentive redhead who smelled like his mom's garden in springtime.

Good grief. She had him reciting poetry now. She wasn't his. His head seemed to understand that perfectly, yet his control over the rest of him hadn't bothered to check the memo.

"Oh, look," Caitlyn announced, pulling out an ornament. "This was Dad's favorite." She held up the Boston Red Sox baseball ornament and pushed a button to make it light up.

His mom nodded then looked away, dabbing at her eyes.

"Sorry, Mom," Caitlyn said. "I miss him, too."

Kennedy cleared her throat. "The holidays are extra hard when you lose someone you love."

"It's true," his mom said, sniffling. "I know it must be hard for you, too, losing your mom not that long ago. It affects everyone this time of year."

Matt gritted his teeth. "Not that Justin seems all that affected."

His mom flinched. "Matthew! How can you say that?"

"Of course Justin is affected," his sister said.

Matt met Kennedy's surprised gaze then had to look away. "It's kind of hard to know that when he's never around," he spat. Tired of hearing his family defend his brother's actions, he dipped his chin and stormed into the kitchen. He needed a breather. If he was forced into spending the night here with Kennedy so close, he might as well make some hot chocolate and drown his misery in sugar.

His mom followed him into the kitchen a few minutes later. She saw him searching the cabinets then shooed him away. "Marshmallows are in the drawer to the left of the microwave," she told him, taking out the bag.

"Thanks," he murmured. He opened it and took out a couple of marshmallows for his cocoa. Hell, he was having a day, and they were tiny, so he dropped in several more.

His mom glanced at his mug and smirked. "That bad, huh?"

"*Yes*, that bad." He took his mug over to the table and sat down.

"Matt, you're not acting like yourself lately. At first I thought you were upset with Kennedy, but now I think it has more to do with Justin."

"Justin and I are okay." Aside from the fact that he

wanted his brother's fiancée. His stomach twisted, and he pushed aside his hot chocolate. "Hell, Mom, I don't know what's going on with me lately."

"Language, dear," she reminded him gently. "Look, you and Justin are different men. I've come to terms with that and have accepted it. I'm not angry with Justin for leaving and working now. In fact, I don't think there's anything wrong with him wanting to better himself and get ahead. Especially when it's so important to him."

"Yes, there's nothing wrong with ambition," he agreed. "Unless it screws up your priorities. Justin hasn't even found the time to buy his fiancée an engagement ring."

His mom sighed. "Kennedy doesn't seem to mind, so why should you?"

He blew out a frustrated breath. "Because family never comes first with him. I'm tired of his excuses, and most of all I'm tired of always making the sacrifices for his benefit." *And man, I'm making a sacrifice now.*

When his father died, who stepped in and took over as head of the household? He did. When Justin just wanted to sell the winery and be done with it, who took over operations? He did. Who gave up his city job and fiancée to move back home to care for his mom and family business? He did. Meanwhile Justin did whatever the hell he wanted and everyone—including Kennedy— seemed to turn a blind eye. So, excuse him for getting a little testy about all that now that he saw the same kind of thing happening with Kennedy. But he figured he was due.

"I thought you loved the winery as much as I do. What do you mean about making sacrifices?"

He shook his head. "Nothing. Forget it."

He *did* love the winery, and it had turned out to be a good decision for him in the end. But he always wondered what would have happened if he had the chance to do the things he had originally wanted to do. If he had taken that job in Boston after he'd graduated, instead of putting aside his dreams to provide for his family. His brother never did appreciate the blood and sweat that went into running Ellis Estates Winery. Then again, it seemed as if Justin didn't appreciate a lot of good things in his life.

Including his fiancée.

"Mom, why are relationships so complicated?"

His mom brushed some hair off his forehead and smiled. "Oh, have you finally met someone?"

"Yes. I mean, *no*. No one."

"Too bad." She clucked her tongue. "It'd be a shame to let one rotten apple spoil the whole bunch."

His lips quirked. "Are you talking about Sam?"

"Don't mention her name," his mom huffed. "I could tell that woman was selfish from day one. She didn't offer to lift a finger once when you first brought her over for dinner. Just sat there like a princess and picked at my good food. I knew right then that I didn't want her to be a part of this family."

Matt chuckled at his mom's outrage. "I would hardly call Sam a princess. Maybe a queen, but not a princess."

"Exactly. What you saw in her besides a pretty face, I'll never know."

Matt thought back on his ex. He wasn't exactly sure what he saw in her, either. They were both so young and at the time had similar interests in movies and music. He didn't really find out about her values and core beliefs until much later. Almost too late. Funny, but he seemed to know a lot more about the kind of woman Kennedy was in a much shorter amount of time.

And she was definitely the kind of woman he could see opening his heart to again. Too bad his brother had met her first.

"I'll never know what I saw in her, either, Mom. But the

point is things worked out for the best there."

"Amen." Her gaze slid to his, and her brows rose mischievously. "Are you sure you aren't bringing this up because you've met someone special? It'd make me so happy to hear you found someone like Kennedy."

Matt doubted that. *Well, actually, Mom, I did find someone like Kennedy. In fact, come to think of it, she* is *Kennedy! Aren't you thrilled?*

He sighed. "No, Mom. And even if I had met someone, now isn't exactly the right time to talk. I'm sure you want to finish decorating the tree, and I just want to go to bed."

"Well, if you ever do want to talk about it, I will always have an ear."

"Thanks, Mom." *But no thanks.* There were some things you shared with your mom, but having the hots for your brother's girl was not one of them.

"Before you go, just try to understand the things that may seem big now are actually very trivial. It's something I've realized since my stroke. Your dad isn't around and I won't be around forever, either. Keep that in mind when dealing with Justin."

He nodded. His mom was right. Here he was supposed to be making peace with his brother and bringing the family together for his mom's sake. Family were the people who were most important. Important enough to make sure old bitterness and some pretty redhead didn't tear that apart.

He enjoyed his job. Liked living on the island. He certainly didn't lack for female companionship when he wanted it. What more could he need out of life? So, he'd put his own wants aside again, content himself with how his life had been going, and be happy for Justin. After all, Justin had been there for him when he'd broken up with Samantha.

Plus, it's what his dad would have wanted. So why did that realization still leave him feeling so hollow inside?

Chapter Nine

Kennedy tiptoed downstairs, making doubly sure not to wake anyone in the house. She was hoping it was just the excitement of decorating the tree that had her still wide awake at two a.m., but she had little faith that her mind could ever be that uncomplicated. No, her thoughts for the last several hours had been on two men and what exactly to do about them. Yes, she still loved Justin, but every time she was in a room with Matt, it was all she could do not to get caught up in the magnetism of attraction that was building between them.

She tried her best to ignore him when they were decorating the Christmas tree, but something would always pull her attention to him. His easy humor. A dazzling smile. The reverent way he treated his mom. What was worse was that he seemed to make no attempt to hide that he was watching her all night as well.

She padded into the living room and couldn't resist flicking the Christmas lights on. The tree was beautiful, full of treasured ornaments that were either made by the Ellis children in grade school or accumulated over the years from places the family had traveled or just events they'd wanted to remember.

Someday, she thought, fingering an ornament made out of Popsicle sticks. Someday, she'd make sure her children had what she never did. Memories. Roots. A real home.

Her mind wandered to Justin and the phone call she'd had with him after dinner.

"Things are actually going great here, Kennedy. You'd be so proud of me. I'm really making the most of this snowstorm and getting a ton of things done at work. I bet they'll make me a branch manager before the new year."

His mention of work had reminded her of her own business and, with dismay, how she hadn't thought of Match Made Easy for almost twenty-four hours. That wasn't like her. She loved her company, valued what she'd created and what she'd felt was her calling in life: to bring people together for a lifetime. Since when had work not become a priority for her?

Since I started to doubt my own matchmaking abilities. That's when, dumb-dumb.

She flicked off the tree lights. Stomach gurgling, she headed toward the kitchen. She turned on the lights and jumped when she saw a figure standing by the window.

"Oh my gosh, Matt," she said, clutching her chest. "You nearly gave me a heart attack. What are you doing up?"

He turned and raised an eyebrow. "I could ask you the same thing."

"Yes, but I wasn't lurking in the shadows ready to send a young twentysomething to an early grave."

He gave her a lazy smile. "I wasn't lurking. I heard a noise and thought maybe it was an intruder. I came downstairs to check it out. It's easier to see out the window without the lights on."

"Oh. It was probably me you heard. Sorry if I woke you."

"You didn't."

No, it didn't look as if she had woken him. His hair barely looked mussed, almost as if he hadn't even bothered getting into bed yet. He had on navy pajama pants and looked to have casually tossed on one of his flannel shirts, leaving it unbuttoned, before he came downstairs. His lean, hard, muscular chest peeked out at her, almost daring her to resist ogling. Knowing she was a weak woman, she decided to busy herself and make some hot chocolate.

"Don't mind me," she said, turning her back to him. "I can't sleep. I'm just going to make myself a little snack." She poured some milk into a mug and stuck it in the microwave.

"Funny, I really couldn't sleep, either. Maybe I'll join you, if you don't mind."

Yes. Yes, she darn well *did* mind.

The last thing she needed was more temptation from the shirtless-wonder himself. She was already a weak woman—and sleep deprived as well. But she took out another mug and filled it with milk. "I don't mind at all," she said with a tight smile.

"Great." He came up behind her, his towering presence all-consuming, and opened a cabinet.

She glanced up, doing her best to keep herself immobile so she wouldn't accidentally touch him. "Oh, so that's where your mom put the marshmallows."

"Yeah, just found out this little secret yesterday."

The microwave beeped. She quickly took her mug out and went to sit at the table. After Matt got done making his cocoa, he joined her. They sipped in awkward silence for several minutes until Matt cleared his throat.

"The Christmas tree looks great," he said, reaching into the marshmallow bag and pulling out another handful.

"Yeah. Too bad Justin wasn't here to help decorate."

His jaw tensed, and his fingers tightened on the handle of his mug. "I guess you...must be missing him a lot, huh?"

She glanced up and found it incredibly hard not to gape at his chest. She jerked her gaze back to her hot chocolate. "Yeah."

"Right. You should. Miss him. What's Christmas without the one you love?"

"Yes, Christmas is an especially nice time to be in a relationship." She bit her lip. "So, uh, why aren't you dating anyone now?"

He shrugged. "No time, really. The winery is pretty busy with baskets and shipments during the holidays."

"Cue the plug for my matchmaking company," she said with a grin. "That's where we come into play. Busy executives, career-oriented business owners, et cetera…with no time to play the field. We could help you. I'll even let you try my matchmaking software for free—as a future family member perk."

He didn't respond for a full minute, and she was tempted to take back the offer.

"No thanks," he finally said. "Do you really think you've cornered the market on relationships because some computer says so?"

"Well…I'm not sure. But I'd like to think so. I *hope* so."

"Why? Why is that so important to you?"

She looked away. "It…it just is."

"No, nothing *just is*, Kennedy. I'd like to know why."

She sucked in her breath, pleased that her chest didn't feel tight despite how distressing the conversation topic was getting. "I just…I don't know. I guess, I don't ever want anyone to go through what my mom went through."

"What was that?"

"Always choosing Mr. Wrong." She laughed, but it was bitter sounding even to her own ears. "My dad left us when I was two or three, so I really don't remember what happened there. But once I got older, I saw a pattern developing. She had no trouble meeting men. My mom was a very attractive woman. But every time she promised me a relationship was going to last, it never did. And when the relationship did eventually fail, she got very, very depressed. It seemed to get worse with each divorce. Things got so bad that I almost had to drop out of college to take on a full-time job to support her."

"But you didn't, so what happened?"

"She met someone. A psychologist in the practice where she was getting treated, actually." She shook her head, remembering how she saw that disaster waiting to happen from a mile away. "Thank goodness, she canceled the wedding two months before they exchanged vows."

Matt blew out a breath. "Well, it does sound as if your mom did have a little trouble in the relationship department."

"To put it mildly. The thing is, she didn't go out to deliberately hurt any of those men or hurt me. She just went with how she was feeling at that moment and never considered anything else. Believe it or not, there are more people out there like my mom than you know." With sinking despair, she realized she might even be one of them. Which was just another reason why she couldn't trust what she was feeling toward Matt.

"So you worked on developing this matchmaking software so people would know these other things to consider before entering into a relationship."

"Exactly. But I'm hoping it'll be a hit for another reason, too."

"What's that?"

"There's another escort/matchmaking company in town that's heavily competing with us. The software is a huge turning point for us." She thought about Mia and all her other loyal employees counting on it—*and* counting on her as well—and her chest grew heavy.

Matt reached out and took hold of her hand. "I'm sorry for making fun of your company before."

"It's okay. You wouldn't be the first to roll your eyes at me about it. Even Justin was a little leery when he first entered our office as a client."

"So Justin came in looking for a quirky redhead, huh?"

"Hardly. But based on how he answered our carefully crafted questions, he definitely gravitated to a more independent, career-minded woman."

He made a face. "With that criteria, I could have fixed him up with my ex-fiancée."

"There's a lot more to it than that, obviously. However, I can't tell you my secret or I'd have to kill you."

His lips twitched. "I would expect no less."

She chuckled then froze when she saw he was still holding her hand. It made her aware of his strength and the warmth of his flesh, and a little shiver ran up her arm. Nonchalantly withdrawing it, she scanned the kitchen counter. "I was hoping your mom would have more Christmas goodies lying around. I'm starving."

"If it took us this long to find the marshmallows, you know we won't find her famous Christmas shortbread until June. That woman knows the best hiding spots."

"Oh, too bad."

"Well, we…we could always make some cookies."

Her head whipped up. "When? Right *now*?" She glanced at the microwave clock. "It's two thirty in the morning."

"It's Christmas Eve. It's the perfect time to make cookies. Unless…you're tired."

She wasn't. In fact, after talking with Matt, she felt strangely energized and alive. Bad feelings to have around your future brother-in-law. She should fake a yawn. Maybe even rub her eyes for good measure. Then bid good night to him. It was the sensible thing to do.

"I'm in," she said instead.

"Great." Matt stood and opened a drawer that held cookie sheets and a rolling pin. "Confession. I've never made cookies before."

She grinned. "Confession. I've never made them, either."

"Oh, this is going to be good. The blind leading the blind," he said with a laugh. He reached up and pulled out the flour and sugar then set them on the counter. "Hey, maybe we need a recipe or something."

Kennedy picked up a bag of chocolate chips and held it out in front of her. "Let's make chocolate chip cookies. The recipe is right here on the bag." She glanced at the directions. "It says we should preheat the oven to 375 degrees."

"What's an oven?"

Her gaze cut to his. "*What?*"

"Kidding!" He walked over to the oven, his eyes shining with subtle humor, and programmed the temperature. "I do happen to live on my own and manage just fine."

She pretended to wipe sweat off her brow. "Good to know."

"Okay, what else do we need?"

She checked the recipe again. "Hmm… two eggs and two sticks of butter. *Softened* butter."

Matt nodded then opened the refrigerator and pulled out the ingredients. After peeling the wrappers off the butter, he placed the sticks in a bowl and set it inside the microwave. "You got to use half a brain to make cookies on the fly like this," he said, tapping a finger to his temple. "We can soften the butter quickly in the microwave."

"Genius," she agreed, folding her arms.

The microwave timer dinged, then Matt pulled the bowl out. He looked at it and frowned.

"Looks like butter soup to me," she said, fighting back a grin.

"Okay, maybe I left it in there too long. I'm sure it'll be fine."

"You mix the butter with the sugar, and I'll measure out all the dry ingredients." She slid the bag of flour over to her, dipped a measuring cup into it, then dumped the contents into a bowl, releasing a cloud of flour dust. She coughed, waving the powder through the air. "Oops."

He pointed and laughed. "You have flour in your hair."

She brushed her head. Then ended up with flour on her nightshirt too. "I'm a mess," she said with a laugh.

"Aw, look at you," he said, patting her on the back. "You're not even hyperventilating. Maybe being around this family long enough, you're getting used to dealing with messes."

She grabbed a towel and smirked. "Yeah, maybe I'm used to them, but it doesn't mean I *like* dealing with them." She gestured to his bowl, which had the finished cookie dough in it. "Looks like you did pretty well without me."

"I don't let messes sidetrack me from my goals. While you were busy cleaning yourself, I was getting down to cookie business," Matt said, scooping out some dough and dropping it onto the cookie sheet.

"A one-track mind, huh?"

He looked over and met her gaze. "Usually."

Unsure how to reply, she turned her attention to helping him scoop dough onto the sheet.

Once he had the sheet full, he placed it in the oven.

"We're ten minutes away from getting that goodness inside us," he said, rubbing his palms together eagerly.

Kennedy went to the refrigerator and poured them each a small glass of milk. It was kind of nice making cookies with Matt. Fun. And not the forced kind. Not that she had anything to feel guilty about there. Family did things like this all the time—although maybe not at three in the morning, alone with their very attractive, single future brother-in-law.

When the timer went off, she grabbed an oven mitt. "Allow me. You practically did all the work, so I'll take them out of the oven."

The cookies smelled heavenly—although they wouldn't win any prize for visual appeal. The dough had spread out and run together in one large, flat blob.

Who cared about how they looked? It was part of the fun, and she was sure they'd taste great.

She carefully placed the tray on a trivet. The cookie sheet started to slide off, and she automatically went to balance it with her other hand, which was bare.

"Ow!" Her left hand began to throb, and she rushed over to the sink to run cold water on it.

Matt was immediately at her side. "Are you okay?"

"I think so." She surveyed her skin under the water. It appeared to be only a minor burn.

"Let me see your hand," he ordered.

She kept it under the water. "Matt, it's fine."

He grabbed her hand anyway and looked himself. "You can never be sure with burns. It could blister before you know it," he said, placing a cool, wet towel off and on it as he inspected her hand.

"Matt, honestly, I'll be fine."

He gingerly brought her hand back under the faucet and let the cool water run over it again. He lifted his gaze to hers, still holding her hand in his. "Are you in pain?"

She shook her head. *Pain? What pain?* she wanted to ask. The way he was holding her hand and treating her as if she were as delicate as crystal wiped any other feelings from her mind. He turned off the faucet but kept her hand in his.

They stood, their gazes locked, for a long moment.

"How do you feel now?" he whispered hoarsely.

Kennedy was too stunned to speak or even move. Her heart hammered in her chest like a woodpecker. If she could form an answer, she would have said she felt dazed, unstable. She licked her dry lips, and his focus caught on her mouth.

"I…" She lost her ability to speak again as Matt leaned closer and lifted a hand to touch her cheek. His eyes seemed to be searching hers for…something. *Permission?* Oh, gosh. He wanted to kiss her. She wanted him to. Terribly. She wanted to feel his lips against hers like she had that day in the elevator. She'd never forgotten that kiss and wanted to relive it for real instead of in her mind. But she held herself in check, still trying to decide what the ramifications of that would entail.

"What are you guys doing?" came a voice behind them. *Caitlyn!*

Kennedy jumped back, banging her hip against the counter. "Nothing!" she blurted.

Ugh. Why did she have to say that? Nothing *always* meant something.

Matt, on the other hand, was the calm, collected one. "We couldn't sleep and decided to make cookies."

"Cookies, huh?" Caitlyn narrowed her eyes as if she were Nancy Drew on a hot case. "Is that what all the commotion was about?"

"I'm sorry," Kennedy said. "I'm so clumsy. I burned myself, and Matt was making sure I was okay."

Her brow furrowed with concern. "*Are* you okay?"

She held up her hand, which was still bright red and stinging. "I'll live."

Caitlyn nodded then eyed the cookie tray. "Well, while I'm up, I might as well join you two. No sense letting warm cookies go to waste no matter what time it is." With a stretch and a yawn, she sat herself at the table.

Matt pulled out a chair and motioned for Kennedy to sit, too. "I'll serve," he said, sounding upbeat, but she thought she caught a hint of regret in his expression before he turned away to grab the cups of milk.

She had regret, too, but a different kind. *What did I almost do?*

The emotions jangling through her—shame, confusion, excitement, anxiety—wouldn't let her sit down and pretend as if all were right between them. *Oh my gosh.* She didn't know what to do with herself, but eating cookies with him and his sister was definitely not it. She thought back on her prior relationships and how they never seemed to last and then, of Justin coming into her life. The one relationship that was perfect. And she'd almost thrown it away.

She slowly backed away from the table. "You know, I think I'm going to head to bed instead."

Matt frowned. "I thought you were hungry?"

She shook her head and gazed at him levelly. "I suddenly lost my appetite."

Chapter Ten

"Babe, you sound funny. Are you sure you're not mad at me?" Justin asked on the phone the next morning. "I know it's Christmas Eve, but I did tell you I'd make it back by Christmas. And I will."

Kennedy rubbed her eyes, then winced when she accidentally put pressure on her burned hand. "No, I'm not upset with you." Truthfully, she was more upset with herself than anything else. She'd almost allowed herself to turn into her mother and ruin a wonderful relationship. "I just didn't get a lot of sleep last night. That's all."

"I know what you mean," he said. "I miss you so much."

"I miss you, too. So you'll be home this morning?" she asked hopefully.

"Not this morning. I have a few things to tie up, then I'll leave. The ferry shuts down early because of the holiday. You should expect me bright and early Christmas morning."

Christmas Day. Her heart thudded.

They had already missed the best part of the holidays together. Plus, another day of him not being here also meant another day she'd have to face his brother. Alone. She wasn't convinced she could.

"Are you sure that stuff can't wait until next week?" she asked. "Maybe we can make cookies if you get home earlier. You know, do some holiday stuff together since you missed decorating the tree."

Justin erupted in laughter. "You are so cute. But you don't need to bother with making cookies. I'm sure my mom has a ton hidden around the house. Besides, I'm bringing home a gingerbread house that one of the partners bought me from that swanky new bakery in the North End. You should see this thing. It's macked out in loads of icing and candy. One taste and you'll forget all about cookies. You know how much I love gingerbread."

Yes, she did know that. Unfortunately, he'd forgotten how much *she* despised gingerbread. "Sounds great, sweetie."

"Awesome. I better go. Can't wait to see you," he added lovingly.

"Same here." She ended the call and remained unmoving on the bed. Justin was arriving on Christmas Day. Not the news she needed to hear at the moment. What she wanted more than anything was to see Justin's handsome smiling face, and have him take her in his arms again so she could feel that nothing had changed between them. That she wasn't making a mistake.

Debating on whether or not to fake an illness and hide out in her room all day, her phone began to ring again. She checked the screen. Mia.

Thank you, God. Work-related news—good or bad— would be an excellent diversion.

"Mia," she answered, "is something wrong?"

Mia chuckled. "Nothing's wrong. In fact, I have good news and decided to call you on Christmas Eve to give you an early Christmas present."

Kennedy sat up. "Good news?" *Finally!* Mia had no idea how much she needed a spirit lift. "What is it? Did Match of the Day declare bankruptcy?"

"Well, no. But there's a very good chance of that happening in the near future."

Mia seemed to pause for dramatic effect.

"Mia! You're killing me with suspense. Just tell me already."

"Okay. Remember when I said I was going to meet with our marketing consultant, a few days ago?"

"Yes…"

"Well, I did. We had a great meeting. Ran through a lot of ideas, and Celeste really seemed to get a sense of what Match Made Easy is and where we see it going in the future. She told me she would get back to us after the holidays with a few proposals, but she ended up calling me this morning with a pitch involving you and Justin that I think you will love."

Kennedy frowned into the phone. "What kind of pitch?"

"Celeste thinks the best time to roll out your software is as soon as possible and not wait until Valentine's Day. She thinks a New Year's Eve press conference announcing the software and your engagement to Justin would be a huge hit. Lots of people will be making their resolutions, resolving to find The One. Plus, a few of the potential investors are holding out because they would like more proof of how happy you guys are and how well the software works. What's better proof than announcing your engagement to the world?"

"On New Year's Eve?"

That was barely a week away.

"Yes!" Mia took a deep breath before continuing on. "They would have a camera crew take some pictures of you and Justin out on the town, celebrating, and get some shots of your kiss at midnight for promo material and maybe even to use in a television commercial. This way they'll have plenty of time and material to put together some outstanding ads for the Valentine's Day rush. Isn't that exciting?"

The walls around her began to close in. Her chest grew tight.

"Yeah, um…" She swallowed. "Wow."

"What's the matter, Ken?" Mia asked nervously. "You don't sound like you're excited."

"No, no, it's not that." Except…it was exactly that. She wasn't as thrilled as Mia was because she felt like a phony—showing everybody how great her matchmaking skills were when deep in her heart, she had doubts about that and about her relationship with Justin. She certainly wasn't ready to announce all that in public.

"Well, what's the matter then?"

"It's just happening so fast. I haven't had a chance to let it soak in. Plus, what if Justin doesn't want to be filmed for TV? He originally only agreed to be mentioned in my software proposal to investors, but not actually be in the ads."

"Don't be silly. Of course he'd want to help you and your business. He knows it's all about getting ahead of the competition. It's just a few pictures. Besides, everybody here is so pumped up. Celeste thinks our stock will go through the roof in a few days just on speculation alone."

"She really thinks this will help the company?"

Mia chuckled. "Help? Celeste thinks you could make Forbes' top ten list of Innovative Companies to Watch."

She had to sit down. Then realized she already was. Ohmygosh, this marketing idea could be the break her little business had been hoping for. She had to go through with this. No matter what. Regardless of her own doubts, too many people were depending on her.

It will be fine. Wouldn't it?

After all, she and Justin were the perfect match. They had to be.

Kennedy drew in a breath. "Okay, I'll talk to Justin tonight about it. In the meantime, tell Celeste we're in and to start planning for it."

"Yay! I knew you'd love the idea! I'll call Celeste now."

"Fine. I'll talk to you in a few days. Merry Christmas, Mia."

"It *will* be a merry Christmas *now*. See ya, boss."

Kennedy hung up, her mind racing. She had to get away from Matt, spend some quality time with Justin. Alone. She couldn't afford another near miss like yesterday's almost-kiss. Knowing what she needed to do, she picked up her cell phone again and hit send. It went straight to Justin's voicemail, but she wasn't surprised. When he was in work mode, he always shut off his cell.

"Hi, honey," she said once his voice message finished playing. "Change of plans due to my work, but I'll explain everything when I see you. So stay in Boston. I'm coming home. See you soon." She hesitated then added, "Love you."

She grabbed her suitcase and started packing. This was the right thing to do. She felt more confident with every piece of clothing she threw in her bag. Justin would understand her leaving his family before Christmas. He always understood *anything* involving business. He might even be thrilled to have her all to himself for the holiday. They could have that time together and rekindle everything she loved about him— without the distraction of his brother.

Her suitcase closed with a final snap. She took it and her laptop case and headed for the stairs.

Mrs. Ellis was rearranging some presents under the tree when Kennedy walked into the living room. "Kennedy," she said, her eyebrows raised, "you look to be going somewhere."

Kennedy inched farther into the room, hating to leave and disappoint her. "I, uh, am. I've had some work-related things come up. I need to get back right away."

Barbara frowned. "But tomorrow is Christmas. Justin will

be back then, and you can always leave the next day together."

If only it were that simple.

"You've been more than gracious having me, but I do really need to get back today." *And as soon as possible.* Before she saw Matt and had to deal with the awkwardness and the hundred different other emotions she felt whenever he was in the same room as her.

Then, speak of the devil, the sound of approaching footsteps came from the kitchen and they both looked over as Matt filled the doorway. Goodness, somehow he looked even better with less than five hours of sleep: wide shoulders, worn-in jeans, his usual flannel shirt, and a baseball cap pulled low.

Her lower abdomen tightened with longing.

He held her gaze for a few intense beats then looked downward at her suitcases. "You're leaving?" he growled. "Why the hell are you leaving on Christmas Eve?"

"Matthew," his mother chided lightly.

She swallowed, barely able to look him in the eye. "Something came up at work. It's kind of important I get back as soon as possible. I left a message for Justin to stay in Boston, and we'll spend Christmas there. Together."

He pulled off his cap and shoved his fingers through his dark hair several times, leaving it in disarray. "Convenient," he murmured.

"For heaven's sake, Kennedy's not a prisoner here," Barbara said. "If she needs to go, then we have to respect that. I'm sure she and Justin will come back to exchange gifts, and we can all celebrate then."

Kennedy let out a relieved breath. She was in the homestretch now. She just needed to call a cab and Google the ferry schedule, and she'd be far, far away from Matt and everything about him that made her feel so out of control.

"Thank you for everything, Barbara. I'm sorry Christmas didn't turn out exactly how you planned." Or *she* planned for that matter.

Barbara walked up to her and wrapped her arms around her. "Christmas turned out wonderfully, because we got to spend time with you. And now I know firsthand what a lovely addition to the family you will make."

Tears stung the back of her eyes. "Thank you," she whispered. Barbara had no idea how much her words meant to her. And how much being loved and included in their family meant. They were everything she ever wanted to have in her life. She couldn't lose them. Because of that, she had to try even harder to make her relationship with Justin work. She took a step back and pulled out her phone. "I should call a taxi to take me to the ferry now."

Barbara placed a hand over her phone. "That won't be necessary, dear."

"It won't?"

"Of course not." She smiled as if Kennedy was a slow-witted child. "Matt will be happy to take you."

"No!" she and Matt said in unison.

"Uh, what I mean," Matt explained, "is the four-wheel drive on my truck isn't working great. Maybe a cab is a better idea."

His mom folded her arms. "Matthew, a taxi is no safer. You need to ride the ferry with her with your car and take her home personally. It's the gentlemanly thing to do in case Justin can't be there to pick her up."

"Oh, I couldn't impose on Matt that way," Kennedy rushed on. "I would feel terrible." *You have no idea…*

"No, I would feel even worse knowing you were traveling all by yourself in this weather and on Christmas Eve no less. Truly, Matt doesn't mind."

Kennedy minded. Big time. This wasn't going along with her plan to stay away from Matt at all.

She hoped Matt had the ability and the good sense to

change his mom's mind. After all, it was for the best that they avoid spending any time alone together from here on out. And by the way the muscle in his jaw was twitching and how he stared down his mother like she was the Grim Reaper, he obviously understood that fact as well.

"I'll go warm up the truck," he said finally, taking her suitcases from her hands.

Oh. My. Gosh. She couldn't seem to get her mind to turn over.

Hazily, she heard his mom speak. "Caitlyn is still eating breakfast if you want to say good-bye to her now."

Kennedy just numbly nodded.

Barbara came up to her and rubbed a hand on her back. "Maybe you should have a snack before you leave. You don't look so well, dear."

Yeah, she didn't feel so well, either.

"I—I just need to see Justin," she croaked. "Then I'll be fine."

She hoped.

Chapter Eleven

Kennedy was quiet the whole ferry trip and most of the car ride to Justin's apartment in the Back Bay. Which was just as well. Matt wasn't exactly in much of a chitchat mood at the moment, either.

In typical Justin-fashion, he hadn't gotten Kennedy's phone messages until late, so he wouldn't be there in time for when the ferry had docked. Instead of letting her freeze half to death waiting for Justin to finally drive down, Matt told her he would take her to Justin's. It wasn't a big deal. He could still drop her off and make the last ferry back onto the island. And the quicker he made it back home, the better. For good reason.

The past week had been hell, trying to resist his attraction to Kennedy.

As he drove through the streets of Boston, his thoughts chased one another through his mind. Thoughts of guilt. Of wanting and trying desperately not to want. He cared about Kennedy. He couldn't help but care about her, now that he'd come to know her better, but there was something more growing between them. He knew by her awkward silence in the car, that she had felt it growing, too.

He found street parking not far from his brother's place. He cut the engine, about to get out of the truck, but her voice stopped him.

"You don't need to see me to the door," she said, not quite meeting his eyes. "You've done enough for me already."

"I'll get your bags and bring them up."

"Matt, really. It's not necessary."

"Well, I know it's not necessary for *you*. However, I might have to use the bathroom. It's a long trip back to the ferry."

She chuckled. "Oh. Sorry. Come on up." She got out of the truck and took her laptop case from the backseat.

Matt grabbed her suitcase and followed. Justin lived in a one bedroom, one bath studio apartment on the eighth floor, which still afforded him a nice view of the city. It looked to be recently updated, decorated in a very clean and contemporary style. After he used the bathroom, he took his time, making an unconcealed effort to check out where his brother was living. He hadn't been up to Boston in a few years.

He heard Kennedy in the kitchen as he picked up a few photographs that were on a shelf. One was of him and Justin and his dad the day Matt got accepted into college. Big grins all around, their arms wrapped together in camaraderie. It saddened him to know that was the last time he and his brother had gotten along. The second photograph was of his mom and Caitlyn when they all had celebrated his sister's thirteenth birthday. He placed them back then looked for others. There weren't any.

Not a single picture of Kennedy.

He frowned as he scanned the room. Besides the suitcase he'd just brought in and the woman herself, there weren't any reminders of Kennedy around. That hardly spoke of a man madly in love. But then again, he and Justin were different men.

Different enough to know that as much as it could hurt his brother, Justin shouldn't be engaged to Kennedy.

"Do you want some tea?" she asked, coming up behind him. "That's all he has. Justin isn't the hot chocolate junkie I am," she said with a self-deprecating smile.

"No. Thank you." He motioned to the room. "How come there aren't any pictures of you and Justin lying around?"

She blinked as if noticing it for the first time. "I…I don't know. I guess we haven't had that many taken together. I'm sure we'll do an engagement picture soon."

"He'll get right on that. Right after he gets you an engagement ring, too, I'm sure," he said, his voice tight.

"I already told you why I don't have a ring yet."

"Yeah, Justin always seems to have some excuse, usually centering around work."

"He's extremely busy now only because he's in the running for a promotion."

He nodded. "I see. And what happens if and when he gets that promotion?"

"Well, I guess we go back to how it was before."

"Before? Like when I met you in Vegas?"

She frowned. "No, not like that. Justin and I worked things out after that time. He promised me he wouldn't let work come between us."

"Oh, of course. And *that* seems to be working out so well."

She stiffened at the sarcasm in his voice. "Matt, you're not being fair."

"Come on, Kennedy, I was engaged to someone just as career-driven. I know exactly what's fair and what isn't."

Kennedy's hands balled together. "I don't understand why you're making such a big deal out of this."

He glowered. "You deserve more. That's all. The man you marry should be putting you up on a pedestal, not treating you as if you were last night's leftovers."

She glowered back. "I'm fine with it."

"I don't think you are, yet for whatever reason you won't admit that to yourself. I've witnessed your hurt and disappointment over the past week. I know it bothered you that you were willing to sacrifice time off from your job, but Justin couldn't do the same. Look, my brother is a great guy, but at some point, you're going to have to come to terms with the fact that Justin is not the man for you."

"Oh, like *you're* the expert matchmaker now. At least I'm not afraid to put myself out there to find love."

"I'm not the expert, but I do have two eyes," he spat. "And no offense, but my brother doesn't act like a man in love. He treats you more like a friend or a close colleague. My God, I've seen him show more attention to my mother's fruitcake than he does to you!"

Her mouth clenched tighter. "So what? Maybe Justin isn't an outwardly affectionate guy. Not every woman is looking for that, you know. And I don't really see what business it is of yours anyway."

"Because it's my business now."

"Since when?"

"Since I've gotten sick and tired of pretending that I don't have feelings for you."

Kennedy gasped. Her mouth hung open. "Oh."

Yeah. Oh.

He hadn't meant to tell her like that, or even tell her at all, but now that it was out there, hovering in Awkward Land, he figured he might as well hammer the nail in the coffin.

Matt ran a hand through his hair before he spoke. "Kennedy, look, I don't want to hurt my brother. It's the last thing my family should have to deal with now, but I need to know if you have feelings for me, because…I think you do."

She opened her mouth, looked about to say something,

then turned away.

He reached out and took hold of her shoulders, slowly turning her around to face him. Her face looked so pale, eyes clouding with tears, and her mind appeared to be going in a thousand different directions. "Sweetheart—"

"Don't call me that!" Her hand went to her chest as if trying to control her breathing. "You…you can't call me that," she said in a more quiet tone.

He held his hands up in surrender. "You're right. I'm sorry. I didn't mean for it to slip out like that. It's just that—for me—what started all those months ago from one kiss in that elevator has grown into something more. I have to be honest." He took a step closer, taking hold of a silky strand of her hair and rubbing it between his fingers. "I don't want to become your brother-in-law. I want to become more than that."

Kennedy didn't say anything for a long minute. He thought she had checked out completely, and he would have to repeat what he'd said, until she finally raised her clear blue eyes to him. "I—I can't," she whispered.

Matt tried to absorb her answer. It wasn't a *hell no*, or an *I won't ever*. It was an *I can't*. That gave him a margin of hope.

"So…does that mean you *do* feel something for me?" he asked warily.

"Yes. I think. I don't know what I feel. Except confused. I—I don't want anyone to get hurt."

He took her hands in his and kissed her knuckles. "Me, either. But I think if we both explain to Justin why you're calling off the engagement, in time he—"

She backed away from him. "I can't call off the engagement."

"What do you mean you can't call it off?"

"Just what I said. I can't."

"But you said you have feelings for another man. *Me*."

"I said I *think* I might have feelings for you." Tears hung in her eyes. "I'm sorry, Matt, but I can't really trust these emotions, a temporary attraction. I can't quite rely on that, not when everything seems to point to your brother."

He snorted. "Your software points to my brother."

"Among other things." She bit her lip. "And my PR firm moved up my software rollout to New Year's Eve. They want a whole publicity circuit centered around me and Justin, so…"

He narrowed his eyes. "Is that all that's really important to you? How your company looks to the media? How very career-oriented of you. So, you're putting your company—ambition—ahead of your heart." Like his ex fiancée had done. Again, he came in second. Well, at least when he fell for a woman he fell for a certain type. *Nice going, buddy.*

"No, it's not like that. It's not just me I'm thinking about. There are a lot of people who are affected by my business. They're counting on me to make this work."

"I hope it does work out for you. Perfectly. Just how you like things, right? Controlled, with no mess. But guess what, Kennedy? I know you don't want to end up like your mom, but people are unpredictable, relationships take work, and life is messy no matter who you are. But I guess I should thank you for turning me on to the real you now before I had really gotten attached, unlike my ex fiancée. I would have hated to have repeated the same mistake twice." He turned to leave. He had to get out of there before he lost it. His chest was on fire.

Kennedy reached out then, wrapped her hand around his upper arm. "Matt, you have to understand. Please don't leave like this."

He understood plenty—that she was ignoring her true feelings and not being completely fair to Justin, either, all for the sake of her business—but was saved from saying anything further when they heard the jangling of keys and then the front door swing open. Justin walked into the living room, dressed in a suit and holding a large bakery box.

"Hey, Matt," he said with a smile. "I didn't expect you. What are you doing here?"

Matt grabbed his jacket and draped it over his arm. "Delivering your fiancée to you. Merry Christmas."

Justin's brow furrowed. He placed the box down on a table and kissed Kennedy on the cheek. A very lame greeting to a fiancée he hadn't seen in more than a week, in Matt's opinion. That dismal display only aggravated him further.

"You're leaving already?" his brother asked. "Why don't you stay and grab dinner with me and Kennedy?"

He almost laughed. "No, that's okay. I need to get back to Mom. Besides, I wouldn't want to impose, especially since you've been apart from Kennedy all week."

Justin swung an arm around Kennedy and grinned down at her. "That's true. Isn't she great? No other fiancée would put up with someone so devoted to his work."

"Yeah. She seems just as devoted to hers, too." His voice broke miserably as his gaze drifted over to Kennedy. "You two are *perfect* for each other."

. . .

Justin had made reservations for Christmas Eve dinner at one of her favorite restaurants in the North End, just the two of them, and then, because she begged him, reluctantly agreed to drive out of the city and stop by Trent's house for dessert.

After her confrontation with Matt, she desperately needed to talk to Maddie. Even with Justin here and Matt gone, she still couldn't stop thinking about Matt or what he'd said to her. Did she not belong with Justin? But how could she back out of their engagement when it hinged on the big media-hyped introduction of their new matchmaking software? Her nice orderly life was in disarray, and she felt as if she were balancing on a tightrope with a sudden case of vertigo.

She could barely eat anything at dinner. Justin remarked on it a few times, but she just brushed it off to having travel fatigue. Once they'd arrived at her cousin's she felt much more at ease when Trent's Old English Sheepdog, Bella, immediately ran up, excited to see her.

"Who's my good girl?" she cooed, rubbing her face and neck. She giggled when the large dog flopped on her back, tongue hanging out of her mouth.

Trent placed his hands on his hips and scowled. "She's *not* a good girl and apparently doesn't realize the strength she has in her tail. The oaf. She's knocked down my Christmas tree four times already since I put it up."

"Hey, she's not an oaf," Maddie said, coming over and rubbing the dog's belly. "Are you, Bella?"

As if to answer, the dog turned and stood so fast, she almost knocked over Justin.

"Oh, yeah," Trent muttered dryly. "She's as graceful as a bull in a china shop."

"Well, *I'm* happy to see her," Kennedy said. "And you, too, cuz. Merry Christmas." She reached on tiptoe and gave her cousin a kiss, then hugged Maddie and handed them a bag of gifts.

"We're so happy you guys were able to come and spend some of the holiday with us," Maddie said, leading everyone into the living room. "It wouldn't have been the same without you. You remember my friends Sabrina and Jack? They're here with their new baby."

Kennedy's mood became even more buoyant. Thank goodness she came home. It seemed as if it'd been months since she last saw Sabrina and Jack. But then again, she'd been so busy with her software development that it probably had been even longer than that.

"Merry Christmas," she said, kissing Sabrina then Jack on

the cheek. "I don't think you guys have met my fiancé yet, Justin Ellis."

As Sabrina and Jack greeted Justin, Kennedy focused all her attention on the little blue bundle in Sabrina's arms. She stroked the baby's cheek, and he gave a little smile. Or maybe he passed wind. Either way, their baby was completely adorable—although hardly surprising when you had two parents as attractive as Sabrina and Jack.

"He's so cute," she gushed. "What's his name?"

"Owen Leonard," Jack said proudly.

Justin, obviously not as interested in babies, sat, and Bella automatically put her head in his lap, which he tentatively pat, trying to avoid getting hair on his suit cuff.

"Kennedy, Maddie was so bummed when you said you wouldn't be here for Christmas that she invited us," Sabrina said with a laugh. "But I'm glad you could make it. I haven't seen you in forever."

"Yeah, it just kind of worked out. Duty called for both of us with work. It turned out we couldn't get away like we originally planned, so we had to come back home."

Maddie tilted her head, spilling blond curls on her shoulder. "Did you get to see your family at all, Justin?"

"Just for an overnight. I'm sure we'll plan something soon enough. But at least Kennedy got some quality time with my family and to do some fun things on the island." Justin looked up and smiled at Kennedy. "My brother Matt was a real lifesaver there."

Yeah. Lifesaver. A wave of panic swept through her. She managed a weak smile back then her gaze cut to Maddie. "Um, do you need help in the kitchen with dessert?"

"Well, I thought we'd sit for—"

"Great! Because I'm starving," she said, dragging Maddie into the kitchen with her.

"Hey," Maddie said, once they were alone. "I thought you

just came from dinner."

"We did. But I could barely eat a thing." Kennedy looked at the counter and almost said a prayer of thanks to the dessert gods. Maddie had made a chocolate mousse—*bless her* for knowing she'd need chocolate—an apple crumble, and a tray of Christmas cookies.

"Wow, you outdid yourself, Maddie. This all looks so good."

Maddie snapped her fingers in front of Kennedy's face. "Focus, Ken. Why couldn't you eat dinner?"

Before she could answer, Sabrina walked into the kitchen. But taking one look at the two of them had stopped her in her tracks. "Uh-oh. Is this a private party or can I listen in? Life with a three-month-old is getting to me. I'm dying for adult conversation that doesn't revolve around poop frequency or sleep *in*frequency."

Maddie raised a questioning eyebrow to Kennedy, who shrugged. "Why not? Misery loves company."

"Ooh, misery talk, yay," Sabrina said, quickly pulling up a stool. "That sounds great."

Kennedy frowned at her.

"Oh. I mean not *great* great," she corrected. "I just mean interesting great."

Maddie rolled her eyes. "Well, I'm interested as to why you couldn't eat dinner, Kennedy."

Kennedy slumped into a stool at the counter and sighed. "Your advice didn't work. Justin is here, and it's all I can do to not think about Matt. Especially after Matt told me that he has feelings for me."

"Oh dear." Maddie slid in the stool next to her. She grabbed a spoon and dug into some mousse. "So what did you say?" she mumbled with her mouth full.

"What could I say? Maddie, you know my background, how my mom was. How can I trust what I'm feeling is real?"

"Honey, you're not your mother."

"I know that." Sort of. But it still wasn't enough to ward off the fears that she'd become like her mom and end up alone with no stability or normal family life. "And then I got the news that my PR firm wants to roll out my matchmaking software early."

"How early?"

"New Year's Eve early. And they want to showcase my relationship with Justin since we were one of the test subjects for it. But how can I say yes if I'm having doubts about my engagement? And if I don't go through with it, my software will be rendered meaningless, investors will pull out, and it'll hurt my company. Mia said some of the print ads already started rolling out."

"Oh dear."

Kennedy flung her hands in the air. "*Please*, stop saying that!"

"I'm sorry! It's like my mouth is on autopilot. I guess I'm having a hard time processing this because it happened so fast."

"Well, I guess not that fast if you count the elevator incident." *Oops.*

Sabrina's mouth dropped open. "See? Now this is the kind of good conversation I'm talking about."

Maddie shushed her friend then put down her spoon. "What do you mean *elevator incident*?"

Kennedy took a few slow, deep breaths. She had told Justin about the man in the elevator in Las Vegas and what had happened; however, she might have left out a few details. Like the man who had kissed her happened to be his brother. And that she might've kissed him back (a little) and had never quite been able to forget it. "I, uh, met Matt before this past week. Ironically enough, it was in Vegas when I was at the Creative Technology Conference."

"Well, what happened in the elevator to make it an incident?"

She cleared her throat. "It got stuck with the two of us on it. You know I don't do well in confined spaces, and he had some wine…and well, we kissed."

Maddie raised her hands to her face. "I'm out of my league here. This is a job for Dr. Drew."

"Maddie, please. You have to understand. It was an accident. And for the record, *he* kissed *me*. But he had no idea who I was." She paused and her mouth hung open. "Ohmygosh, all this time I've been worried about becoming my mother. I already *am* my mother."

"Relax, honey. You haven't done anything." She peered at her more closely. "Did anything else happen between you two when you went to visit Justin's home?"

"Gosh, no! We would never hurt Justin like that. But even with Matt out of the picture, I'm not sure how I feel about Justin anymore. How did you know Trent was the one?"

"Well, it was hard to know at first. I thought I was cursed in the relationship department. But I realized by holding onto that belief, I wasn't allowing myself to take that leap of faith. Nothing is an absolute sure thing."

She looked to Sabrina. "How did you know Jack was the one?"

Sabrina bit her lip. "Technically, not until I got engaged to another man. When that happened, I realized I only had companionship but not a real connection with him. It helped me see that with Jack, I truly had both. Plus, I had a little psychic help."

Kennedy hung her head, willing herself not to cry.

"Look, honey, everyone has their own story and their own wants. I don't think you should look to Trent or me or Sabrina and Jack for advice. You should look inside yourself and see what you truly want, what will make you the happiest, before you make any decision."

She nodded. "I'll try."

"Okay, but I wouldn't waste time. New Year's Eve is in five days, you know."

"Hey!" Trent called from the other room, "I thought dessert was coming. Do you girls need any help?"

"No, we're good," Maddie called back. She gestured for Kennedy to pick up the plate of cookies. "We're coming now."

Kennedy willed herself back into control and followed Maddie into the living room. She placed the cookies out of Bella's reach and sat down next to Justin. He automatically wrapped an arm around her and squeezed her shoulder. She waited for it. The little zing of attraction. Nothing. Matt only had to look at her and her knees turned to melted ice cream. Although she couldn't ever remember experiencing that with Justin. Just comfort and ease. She hadn't seen Justin all week, so shouldn't she be feeling *something* besides annoyance with herself?

Just when Kennedy already felt at her lowest, she saw Sabrina lean down and plant a loud kiss on Jack's lips as he cradled the baby in his arms.

"What was that for?" he asked, smiling at his wife.

Sabrina shrugged. "Just feeling extra fortunate to be married to you."

"Would it help *my* good fortune if I were to inform you that I changed Owen's diaper while you were in the kitchen?" he asked, waggling his eyebrows suggestively.

Sabrina cocked her head, pretending to think it over. "Not sure. Was it a number one or a number two?"

"*Two*." Jack fake shuddered.

"You just earned extra bonus points tonight, buddy." Sabrina kissed her husband again, and their baby began kicking his legs.

Chuckling, Maddie handed out plates then sat down next

to Trent. "All right, enough you two. Owen looks like he's getting gassy over his parents frequent PDA. Hey, why don't we open gifts?" she suggested.

Kennedy perked up. That actually sounded like a pretty good idea. Something fun. She reached for the bag she'd brought and pulled out a gift for Trent. "Here ya go. For the cousin who has everything." She then pulled out a bone for Bella, who happily took it from her hand and ran off.

Trent shook the box with extra care then, apparently deciding there was no bomb, began opening it. When he saw the contents, his face split into a wide grin. Kennedy almost laughed when he held the nine-inch replica of the stadium where he'd played football in college as if it were a newborn. "Aw, Ken, how in the world did you pull this off?"

Kennedy winked. "Justin and I have our connections."

"Thank you."

Justin cleared his throat. "I'd actually like to give my present next."

Kennedy took a cookie and bit into it. "What are you talking about? That was from both of us, silly."

"No, actually. I'd like to give a present to *you*."

She almost choked. "I, uh, didn't bring a gift for you. I thought we would exchange tomorrow."

"I know." He pulled out a small black box with a red bow from the inside of his suit jacket. "This one can't wait," he said with a shy smile.

The box fit in her palm yet sat in her hand as clumsily and as heavy as a microwave. Mixed feelings surged through her. She looked into his kind hazel eyes, hesitating for a brief moment, then opened it. An engagement ring sat shining and ready to wear.

"I know it's not the traditional kind," Justin rushed to explain. "I didn't think you'd really care about stuff like that. It's just when I saw it, I thought the ruby suited you."

Kennedy was more of a traditional kind of girl, but the fact that he went out and picked a ring for her with such care and thought warmed her insides. *This is right*, she thought. Justin was everything she wanted, so why wouldn't he still be now?

Realizing she had kept Justin and the rest of the room in suspense for too long, she finally turned to him with a huge grin. "It's what I always wanted."

"Are you sure?" he asked.

She glanced at Maddie then blinked back tears. Ignoring her friend's worried stare, she told him, "It's perfect."

But would she ever be able to shake the feeling that while the ring was perfect, the man might not be?

Chapter Twelve

"Kennedy, the makeup artist over there thought it'd be a good idea to *de-glow* you now."

Kennedy gave Mia a pointed glare. "Look, I know I'm sweating like a tennis player at Wimbledon, so spare me the decorum."

Mia chuckled. "Sorry, boss. I know you're nervous today, but you're going to knock 'em dead at the press conference. Just remember, Celeste wants to run through a few things with you before you go on, okay?"

Kennedy nodded, trying to take in a few deep breaths. She hadn't seen Justin since Christmas Day. Didn't even spend the whole holiday with him, instead feigning sickness—which hadn't exactly been a lie. Matt's words had haunted her.

I know you don't want to end up like your mom, but people are unpredictable, relationships take work, and life is messy no matter who you are.

Well, she certainly had made a mess out of her life. How had she let this happen?

And even if she succumbed to her feelings for Matt, it

wasn't like they could just begin to see each other. That could very well tear Justin and his family apart. There were no clear-cut answers. Maybe it was just her. Maybe she wasn't trying hard enough in her relationship with Justin because she was too consumed with Matt. She had to make it right between them like it had been—for herself as well as her business.

"I'm going to attend to the press," Mia told her. She gave her another reassuring smile. "You'll feel better once you see Justin's smiling face in the audience."

She nodded. "I know. Thanks."

A few of her employees passed by and waved. "Good luck, Kennedy!" one of them called.

She smiled and waved back. *For this rollout to be a success, I'm going to need that luck.*

Celeste, their marketing consultant, came barreling over to her with her trim gray suit and upswept platinum hairdo. "You ready, Kennedy?"

Kennedy had rehearsed her speech all week until she could recite it in her sleep. *Please.* Press conferences and speeches she could do standing on her head. It was one of the reasons her employees were so confident in her. Relationships, on the other hand... She obviously needed more help than her own company could supply. "As ready as I'll ever be."

"Great. I'll talk about Match Made Easy a bit first, and then the software, then I'll introduce you and you can talk more about it, and the exciting results you've gotten with your own engagement."

"Right." Her chest tightened.

"Okay, see you in ten minutes."

As Celeste walked off on her gray four-inch stilts, Kennedy's cell phone went off. She checked the screen and saw it was Justin.

"Hey, honey," she greeted. "We're in the conference center on the third floor. You've still got—"

"Babe, that's why I'm calling. I'm running late."

She held in a sigh. "Oh, no, Justin, really?"

"Aw, hon, don't worry, you don't need me there. You're a powerhouse CEO. You're going to slay the competition today."

"I know, but I really wanted you here for moral support."

"Babe, know that I'm thinking about you. I'll be over there as soon as I can, and we can have the rest of the night together celebrating. I'll make sure our pictures for the photo op look their best, too. I've made super secret reservations tonight. Your favorite wine is probably chilling as we speak."

That coaxed a small smile from her. "You don't need to chill pinot noir, silly."

"Pinot noir? No, I ordered a few bottles of prosecco for us."

Prosecco? She didn't like prosecco. Sparkling wine gave her indigestion. How could Justin not remember that? Then Matt's words began to ring in her head. *You deserve more.*

She'd once thought she couldn't be luckier to find a man like Justin, someone steady, a companion who shared her love for details and order, not to mention TV shows. Not so long ago, she couldn't imagine what she had done in a previous life to deserve him. But now, she had to wonder if he truly deserved *her*, and her heart grew heavy at that thought.

So that was it. Matt was right.

She now knew she couldn't go through with the engagement. Actually, she'd known it for a while, but not until this very minute had she been able to admit the truth.

"Justin," she whispered, her voice breaking, "I—I'm sorry. I don't think this is going to work."

"It'll be fine, Ken. I can switch the prosecco to pinot noir."

She closed her eyes and sighed. "No. It's not the wine. It's us. *We're* not working. I thought we could. By all accounts we *should*, but— "

"I know, babe. I know I said I'd be better about my work schedule, but I promise things are going to be different once I get my promotion. So you do your thing, and I will hands down be there for you tonight. Just be patient with me for a little longer. We'll talk about it when I see you, okay?"

"No, Justin, you're not listening—"

"What?" he asked, but he wasn't talking to her. He was talking to someone he was in the room with. The irony was unfortunately not lost on her. "Sorry, Kennedy. I need to go. I have a client on the other line. But I'll see you tonight."

"No—" Words failed her. Not that it mattered anyway. He had already hung up.

Hands shaking, she headed for the bathroom—an area she hoped she could quietly compose herself in. She steadied herself against the sink and tried to even her breathing. She had thought Justin, of all people, understood what an important day this was to her, to her business. After all, they were like-minded when it came to their careers. She supposed there were no more excuses to be made. Nothing left to talk about. He had made promises and failed to keep them. As Matt had told her, they did not act like two people head over heels in love with each other.

Today more than ever, she wished her mom were still living. She may not have had much of a family life, but her mother *was* her family. Trent had been wonderful, but for so long, it had just been the two of them. And without her—and especially now without Justin—Kennedy felt very much alone. As much as it pained her to admit defeat in her relationship with Justin, she did deserve more. And maybe that's what her mom in all her dismal marriage attempts was really searching for. Something more.

She stood there in the eerie silence of the women's room, trapped in the lie she'd been telling herself for months, and looked at herself in the mirror. She winced when she saw how pale she was. *Some powerhouse CEO.*

I can do this. I know the software is a success—even without being engaged to Justin.

She glanced down at her hand, staring at the ring that Justin had thoughtfully picked out for her. Would everything be fine if she and Justin just sat down and talked, worked out some of the bugs of their relationship? Justin seemed to think so, but too much had happened. Things weren't as perfect as they'd been. Not since before she'd visited his family. Not since well before she'd met Matt.

Glancing at the time, she spun around and headed out the door. And ran smack dab into Matt.

A jolt of pure joy coursed through her.

"Matt!" she said, sliding her glasses back up her nose. Oh, he was a sight for sore eyes. He wasn't wearing his standard flannel shirt today, but a sports jacket and jeans, with a thin cranberry sweater that molded to his chest muscles. It had only been a few days since she'd seen him last but he looked... so much more handsome than she remembered.

Matt stared at her, unblinking. He still had his hands on her shoulders, steadying her as if he was afraid she was about to collapse.

"Wh-what are you doing here?" she asked.

"I felt bad about how we left things. Listen, I don't agree with everything that you're doing but I had some time to think about you and Justin, and I had no right to say the things I did. You were right. It's none of my business. You're the matchmaker. Anyway, I know today is an important day for you. I figured you'd want family—or at least soon-to-be family here."

Thank goodness Matt still had his hands on her because her knees did a little wobble.

"You came all the way out here for me?" Her lips began to tremble.

He reached up and took her face in his hands. "Hey, no tears. Please," he said gently. "If I had known I was going to smear your makeup, I would have stayed home."

She chuckled. "I'm glad you didn't. I'm sorry for how we left things, too. I was awful to you."

Matt dropped his hands, took hold of hers, and squeezed. When he did, his brows furrowed, and he raised her left hand to inspect it. "Well, well, looks like my brother pulled through after all. You were right again."

"Oh. Yes." Her cheeks heated, and she withdrew her hand from his. "He surprised me with an engagement ring on Christmas Eve."

He stared at it as a muscle worked along his jaw. "It suits you. The ruby. Your red hair. Looks like everything is snapping into place for you." He raised his gaze to hers. "Just like you wanted."

"Yeah…" She bit her lip. *Not exactly how I wanted. I may have picked the wrong brother.*

Mia came running over to her then, grabbing her arm. "Kennedy! Celeste is going to introduce you any minute now."

Kennedy blinked. "Oh, right." *The press conference.* Where she was supposed to tell the world how happy she was with her match—with her soon-to-be wedding. But instead, her instincts urged her to grab onto Matt's shirt and not let go.

He stepped back. "Your job strikes again." And just like that it became all about her choosing her job over him again.

"Matt, I have to do this."

"I'm sure you do."

Mia tugged. "Come on."

Kennedy glanced back at Matt one last time. His gaze seared into hers. "You better go do your thing," he said tightly. "They're counting on you."

Right. All feelings aside, she had people counting on

her to sell their product. It was her job. Why couldn't Matt understand that? She sighed then let Mia whisk her off to the conference room.

The room was filled. There was a cameraman in the corner and several reporters as well as many of her staff in the audience. She recognized a few clients and some of the test group couples. As she passed Trent, he mouthed, *You got this*. If he meant she had the stomach flu, she wouldn't have disagreed. Balls of nausea were swirling in her gut like tumbleweeds. But she pasted on a confident smile once she approached the podium.

Celeste grinned back and sent her a subtle right-on-time nod. "Match Made Easy holds a firm belief that love is the very best part of life, and therefore you owe it to yourself to find the very best matchmaker. Its unique style of personalized service is second-to-none. And by unique, I mean that Match Made Easy holds the patent to a brand-new software program specifically designed to help people successfully navigate the modern dating world. With more on her program and how it will forever change the status of future relationships, I am very honored now to introduce to you the mastermind behind this wonderful company, Kennedy Pepperdine."

Applause broke out around her as she humbly took center stage. She shook Celeste's hand then turned to face the audience. She gazed up, and that's when she zeroed in on Matt standing way in the back of the room. Something clicked in her mind then. Matt had shown up to support her rollout, even though he was not a fan of her software or her marketing ploy. Matt was always there for those he cared about: his mom, his sister, even Justin. And he seemed to truly care about her—and had not only told her with words, but went out of his way to *show* her as well. She never got a fraction of that with Justin.

I think you deserve more.

Yeah. She did. But since she couldn't have Matt, she did deserve something else. Self-respect. She had already been honest with Justin, but now she needed to be honest with herself and the people willing to use and/or invest in her company.

Suddenly looking concerned, Matt gave her a thumbs-up sign to encourage her to start speaking.

That was all she needed to see.

She cleared her throat. "Thank you all for coming out today. You know, Match Made Easy is an extraordinary company because we really love what we do. We love bringing the right people together and having it last. That was the main reason I worked for so long to get this matchmaking software to exactly where I wanted it to be. Relationships are to be treasured, and I didn't want there to be mistakes. But I wanted our clients to have it easy and simple, and well... perfect. So of course, I had to try it out on myself first." There were a few laughs in the audience. "And I *did* find the perfect match for myself."

She held up her hand to show her engagement ring, and some of the audience *oohed* and *ahhed*. "Yes, I even got engaged to a wonderful man. We tried our matchmaking program on our test group soon after that, and it came back with a ninety-nine percent matchmaking accuracy report." More applause sounded. "Yes, I'm thrilled with those results, and I'm very proud of what we can do for people. But...as someone recently told me, relationships take work, people are unpredictable, and life is always messy. And, unfortunately, I couldn't plug all those things into a computer software system."

The room went silent. Celeste came and stood next to her with an embarrassed smile, looking like she wanted to yank away the microphone along with a handful of Kennedy's hair, but Kennedy wasn't nearly finished.

"So as proud as I am of my software and how it can help couples, it really can only bring them so far. The rest is up to them—and maybe a little bit of chemistry. Because of that, I also sadly have to announce today that my engagement is off."

Commotion and questions erupted from the audience. The sound was chaos, and everything became a blur. Two hands grabbed her by the shoulders and yanked her away from the podium as Celeste stepped up to the microphone.

"I'll be happy to answer any questions," Celeste barked into the microphone. "Miss Pepperdine might have spoken in haste about her upcoming marriage, so until we find out the true story, please refrain from any questions about her relationship."

Mia wrapped an arm around her and quickly ushered her to a side room to escape the cameras. Her emotions frazzled, Kennedy managed one last glance back to search the room.

But Matt was nowhere in sight.

. . .

Back in the confines of her office, Kennedy sipped an herbal tea—that tasted neither *special* nor *relaxing* as the wrapper indicated—that Trent had brought her to soothe her nerves. He also brought her a fresh paper bag, the sweetheart. Thank God he was there with her, because she needed the extra support. She knew she'd blown it today at the press conference, but she had to be honest with everyone, and she needed to be honest with herself. It's what her clients should expect. Celeste, however, and a few of her PR assistants were on the warpath.

"*You,*" Celeste said, pointing her red-nail-polished finger at her, "completely sunk your own company, and we won't be held responsible."

Trent stood and blocked her finger. "Hey, now. Nobody said anything about pointing blame at anyone. Besides, we were all there. Kennedy was nothing but honest and spoke from the heart."

Celeste snorted. "Well, from now on, she's going to be speaking from the unemployment line."

Kennedy's shoulders slumped. She may have spoken from her heart, but she may also have ruined her business and the lives of everyone working for her.

"I'm sorry," she said lamely. "I know I ruined everything. All I ever wanted was to bring people together and make them happy, but it seems as if all I've done is bring misery— mostly to myself. But I've been having doubts for a while about me and Justin, and well, when I saw Matt here today, I knew I couldn't go through with the press conference."

"Wait. Who's Matt?" Trent asked.

"My *brother*," Justin announced from the doorway.

Kennedy had never seen Justin anything else but well-groomed, easygoing, and well, pleasant. But standing in her office, he looked like a caged lion sprung free. His tie was crooked, and his suit jacket was completely disheveled as if he'd thrown it on in a mad rush. The top of his blond hair stood up slightly as if he had run both hands though it many times over.

"Justin," Kennedy whispered. "What are you doing here? I thought you said you couldn't make it."

"Well, after I just learned on the local news that my fiancée broke off our engagement, I figured I'd better get down here and find out what's going on. Is this some sort of publicity stunt?" he said, chest heaving.

She wished.

She shook her head sadly. "I tried to tell you earlier on the phone. But you wouldn't listen. I'm really sorry, Justin. I can't imagine what your mom and sister must think of me. I didn't want anyone to get hurt."

Justin snorted. "A little late for that."

Trent made the time-out sign. "Maybe you guys should deal with this without an audience," he said, motioning for Celeste and her crew to head out.

Celeste's mouth was grim, but she grudgingly picked up her portfolio and made her way to the door. "I guess I'll go and see if there is any damage control that can be done."

After Trent made sure everyone was out, he sent Kennedy a sympathetic shrug and closed the door behind him.

Justin sighed, pinching the bridge of his nose. "Does you not wanting to get married to me have anything to do with Matt?"

She hesitated. "Just a little," she admitted.

"Did he touch you? Did he do anything to you? That son of—"

"*No*. Honest. He was a perfect gentleman. I—I just don't think you and I are right for each other."

His angry demeanor fizzled before her eyes. "But why? We're so similar. We want the same things out of life. I love you. And your software said we were perfect for each other, too."

Kennedy closed the gap between them, laying a hand on his forearm. "Yes. All that is true. And we *are* perfect for each other. On paper. In real life, not so much. Relationships take work, and neither of us is willing to do that. You couldn't even find the time to spend our designated holiday vacation with me."

His face registered blank surprise. "But you never complained. Not really."

"No, I never did. I had hoped things would change. Actually, I think I never told you a lot of things that bothered me because I didn't want to rock the boat and mess our relationship up. I *wanted* it to be perfect. And for a while, I convinced myself it really was."

"I thought it was."

"We were both busy and looking for the easy solution to being single. But honestly, Justin, you deserve better, too."

Justin hung his head, looking like a little boy who dropped his ice cream. "I wanted this to work," he said finally.

She thought of the rest of the Ellis family, how much she'd miss them, and a new anguish seared her heart. "I know. You like neat and tidy just as much as I do," she said with a half smile.

Then she lifted her left hand and slid her engagement ring off. With a lump in her throat, she held it for him to take.

He reached out and took it between his fingers, giving her a smile that didn't quite reach his eyes. "Not that I imagine it would have changed things, but you know, it might have made things easier for you, so for what it's worth, I am sorry I wasn't here for you today. I'm sorry I wasn't there for you a lot of days."

A tear slid down her cheek. "Me, too."

Chapter Thirteen

"I had a feeling you'd show up."

Matt had prepared himself for his brother's frosty tone. His fiancée had just broken up with him in front of a crowd of people on local television. Matt's name had never come up during the announcement, but he had to imagine that if Kennedy was going to be honest in public, she was going to be honest to Justin about her and Matt's attraction to each other.

Matt had left the press conference shortly after Kennedy announced she was breaking off her engagement to his brother. Once the uproar began, he felt it was his duty to call his mom and explain—explain as much as he could, anyway— just in case she'd been watching the news or Caitlyn had heard it through one of her social media outlets. His mom was upset, naturally. She had grown attached to Kennedy over that short amount of time.

They all had.

"So what are you doing here?" Justin asked.

"I heard about your broken engagement to Kennedy. I'm sorry."

Justin snorted. "Are you?"

"Yes, I *am* sorry." No matter their differences or their apparent similar taste in women, the last thing he wanted was to see his brother hurt.

Justin gazed at him for a long moment then simply turned and walked back into his living room.

Matt stepped in, closing the apartment door behind him, then followed his brother.

Justin sat back on the sofa, propping his feet up and going back to watching TV. Several empty bottles of beer lined his coffee table like soldiers waiting at attention. Matt shook his head and sat down. His brother even drank neat and organized. Matt supposed his brother and Kennedy did share similar anal traits, in that regard.

"What the hell happened at home while I was away?" Justin asked, staring straight ahead.

"Nothing happened."

Justin's gaze cut to his. "Well, *something* had to have happened! Your fiancée doesn't just change her mind about marrying you on a whim. Everything was so great and now…"

"Was everything great, Justin?"

"*Yes.* Yes, it was perfect."

"Perfect, how? To you? Because you finally had a relationship where you could concentrate on your job and maybe—just maybe—when you had a free moment to spare, you had a woman in the background so you wouldn't be lonely? Good grief, Justin, you have the same priorities with women as you do with family. Do you honestly blame her for wanting more?"

"Hey, don't go bringing family into this. You never understood what it was like to be second best—especially in Dad's eyes. Why do you think I work so hard?"

"Justin, nobody loves you because of what you're doing or achieving. We love you for you. When you're around, that is. But you never are. You never seem to take responsibility for anything at home. Mom does a good job of hiding her feelings, but I can tell it's wearing on her—which wears on me."

"I know." He shook his head. "I just want Dad to be proud."

The despair etched on his brother's face weighed heavily on him, but Justin had to hear the truth. "He'd be prouder if you didn't treat Mom and the rest of the family as an afterthought," he said gently.

Justin rubbed a hand over his face. "Are you saying my priorities are screwed up?"

"I would have probably said it a little more colorfully, but yes."

"I know." He sighed. "After Dad died, I just kind of checked out. I'm sorry if I wasn't around to help you with Mom and Caitlyn and everything."

Matt dipped his chin.

Justin blew out a breath. "I guess I can't really blame Kennedy for breaking off our engagement. I thought I could fix things between us, but our relationship was never quite the same since her trip to Vegas for that technology conference."

Vegas. Matt looked up at his brother. Swallowed hard. Kennedy had the confidence to be completely honest today, and now he felt he owed Justin that much as well. "I, uh, heard Kennedy had an incident with a guy kissing her in an elevator out there in Vegas," he hedged.

"She told you about that?"

Matt shook his head. "She didn't have to… I was that guy."

"*You* were the one who kissed Kennedy? Ah, hell, Matt. Well, that explains why she was acting more anxious than normal when I brought her home to meet everyone. What the hell were you thinking?"

"I wasn't thinking! I mean, I was, but obviously I didn't know she was yours."

"That's right. She *was* mine," he snapped.

"Right. Sorry again."

Justin stood then walked over to a window that offered a view of Boston Common. After a few silent beats, he turned around. "So...tell me, do you have a thing for Kennedy or something now?"

Matt would hardly call what he felt for Kennedy a mere "thing." But on the other hand, it was too new and unknown to be identified as anything else. He hesitated a moment, not wanting to hurt his brother any more than he already was, but he still felt the need to be upfront. "I do like her," he admitted.

"*Like* her like her?"

"For Pete's sake, Justin, have we not expanded our dialogue beyond grade-school recess talk?"

Justin sadly nodded. "I think I got my answer. I also think it's time for you to go," he said, walking toward the door.

Matt got up and followed his brother's lead. At this point, even though things weren't finished between him and Justin, there couldn't be any more said tonight. He needed to catch the last ferry back onto the island, too. Mom and Caitlyn were probably still reeling from the news.

Justin unhooked his leather jacket from the coat hanger, fixing Matt with a long, tired stare, and dangled it from his index finger. An awkward silence followed.

Matt's throat suddenly tightened. He hated leaving things this way. Hated leaving his brother alone now. He seemed so broken. "Look, I—"

Justin landed a punch squarely in his jaw, causing Matt's head to snap back and hit the wall. Pain exploded in his face and for a few seconds he could barely see straight. His brother did always have a mean right hook.

He slowly raised his hand to cradle his throbbing jaw. "I

suppose, in some way, I deserved that."

Justin swung open the door. "Yeah, you did."

• • •

Kennedy took the spoons out of the freezer and carefully placed them over her eyelids.

After crying herself silly once she got home from today's press conference fiasco, she'd Googled how to get rid of puffy eyes, and so far it seemed to be doing an okay job.

What was Matt up to tonight? She wondered if he'd stayed in town or went back home to go out with friends. It was probably for the best that she hadn't seen him after announcing that her engagement to his brother was off. That water was muddy enough. She understood about family loyalties. She couldn't expect him to go and betray that loyalty for her.

She removed the spoons and grabbed herself a bottle of wine off the counter then went into the living room. Clicking on the TV, she got ready to settle in for a night of *Dick Clark's Primetime New Year's Rockin' Eve*. The irony wasn't lost on her that for heading up one of the premiere matchmaking/ escort companies in the state, she did not have a date for New Year's Eve.

Maybe that was a sign she should get out of matchmaking.

Just as she was about to pour herself a glass of wine, her cell phone rang. Thinking it could be Matt, she rushed to answer it only to get her hopes deflated by the name on the call screen.

"Hey, Mia," she answered, without emotion.

"Um, hello to you, too," she said with amusement in her voice.

"Sorry, but I just don't have the energy to hear all the problems I've created for the company or to hear the list of complaints Celeste has with me right now. Spoiler alert: I know I messed up."

"Honey, relax," Mia told her, "Celeste and her crew did some talking to the press and even to some of our test subjects. And you know what? People actually responded really well to your honest and upfront approach to dating and relationships."

Kennedy straightened so fast, she almost knocked over her wine. "They did?"

Mia chuckled. "I know. Celeste couldn't believe it, either. But she managed to spin their response in such a way that you already have an offers to do interviews for *Boston* magazine and *Cosmopolitan*. Ken, I think we're going to be okay."

Kennedy breathed out a huge sigh of relief. "Oh thank God, I don't know what I would have done if I had failed you guys."

"Ken, it's okay. I know it's your company, and you started it, but there are a lot of people who are grateful for the opportunity you've given to them working for you. Me included. And we wouldn't let you go down with the ship alone. We would have done everything in our power to help. To help you. It's like family to us."

Like family. Hearing that, and that she wasn't alone in trying to keep her company afloat, lifted her spirits. "Thanks, Mia. I needed to hear that."

"I know you did. But I just wished you would have been upfront with me on your hesitations about Justin. I would never have pushed the marketing campaign so hard if I had known."

"You're right. I'm so sorry. From now on, I promise to keep you more informed with the business."

"Good. So maybe you can dial down the anxiety and not need your paper bag so much now?"

"Whoa, whoa, that's like asking Linus to just give up his

blanket cold turkey. Let me get my life back together and then we'll talk."

"Okay." Mia chuckled. "And Ken, I am sorry to hear about you and Justin."

"Thanks."

"I really thought you two belonged together, but I guess if you want to be happy, you have to go with your heart, huh?"

Kennedy smiled to herself, thinking about her mom. "Yeah, I guess you do have to follow your heart."

There was a sudden knock at the door.

"Gotta go," Kennedy said, grabbing the twenty she had on the coffee table. "My pizza is here. Happy New Year's." Clicking off the cell phone, she went to the door.

And found Maddie and Trent standing in the hallway. Kennedy pasted on a smile. "Oh. Hey. Shouldn't you guys be out celebrating the holiday?" She winced at how pathetic her attempt at upbeat sounded.

Maddie's eyes filled with sympathy. "We didn't want you to spend New Year's alone."

Trent held out his beefy arms, and she practically jumped right into them. They knew her so well. Thank goodness she didn't have to be alone. She loved them both so much she thought her heart would explode on the spot. Even if she wasn't marrying Justin and wouldn't have the Ellis family as a part of her life, she would always have Trent and Maddie. And they were the best family to have.

"Thank you," she mumbled into her cousin's chest. "If you hadn't shown up, I'm sure I would have eaten an entire pizza by myself. Probably an entire sleeve of Fig Newtons, too. And a bag of stale Doritos."

"See, Trent? I knew we should have come over sooner. Maybe even have taken her out."

Kennedy backed out of Trent's arms and slid her glasses back up her nose. "No, no. I definitely don't want to go out.

Come on in."

Maddie took off her coat then handed her a wrapped package. "Here. This is for you."

"What's this?" she asked, inspecting the outside of the box. "I thought we already exchanged Christmas gifts."

Trent shrugged. "It's not from us. It was sitting outside your door when we got here."

"Really?" She glanced at the card.

Kennedy: I thought you could use the reminder. M-

Matt. She hesitated briefly then tore open the wrapping. Inside there was a simple blue T-shirt, with a message on the front that read: *The only certainties of life are 1) that it's not perfect and 2) that it's messy.*

Maddie frowned at the shirt. "Interesting gift."

"Yeah." Kennedy sniffed and folded it back into its box. "Private joke."

"Is it from Matt?"

Not trusting her voice, Kennedy nodded.

"I'm sorry things didn't work out for you," Maddie said.

"I'm not," Trent added. "I never thought Justin was right for you."

Kennedy drew back and tilted her head. "Yeah. You mentioned that. Why did you feel that way?"

"Men's intuition." When Maddie rolled her eyes, he shrugged. "What? You women think you've cornered the market in that area? Plus, you and Justin were way too similar. Too perfect. He seemed more like a brother to you than a potential husband. I think you need friendship, but there has to be a spark, too."

Maddie gaped at her future husband. "You, Montgomery, are turning into an old softy." Her lips grew into a mischievous smile. "And I like it."

Her cousin grabbed Maddie's hand and pulled her onto

his lap. "Well, if you like that, I'd be happy to go over a few more of my relationship theories tonight," he said, burying his face in her neck, causing Maddie to giggle.

Kennedy waved in front of them. "Uh, hello? Can you guys give it a break for a few hours and *not* advertise how happy you are? Because I have to be honest, it's not really helping."

Maddie's cheeks colored as she slid off Trent's lap. "Sorry."

Kennedy sighed. "Don't be. If anything, you've solidified my breakup with Justin. There wasn't much of a spark." Not like she had with Matt, anyway.

As if picking up on her thoughts, Maddie asked, "Have you heard from Matt?"

Kennedy pointed at the gift. "Only through this. Not that I really expected to hear from him anyway. I broke his brother's heart, I probably caused his mom to have another stroke, and I'm sure his sister is using the sweater I bought her for Christmas as guinea pig bedding. He could only hate me as well," she said miserably.

Maddie laid a hand on her shoulder. "If that was true, he would have never left you that Christmas gift."

"He probably couldn't return it," she murmured.

"So what are you going to do about this guy?" Trent asked.

Her eyes widened. "Seriously? I came in like a wrecking ball to his family. What do you expect me to do? Send an oops-my-bad candygram?"

Trent's lips tightened. "How about picking up the phone and calling him?"

"No. He made it perfectly clear how he felt when he rushed off before the press conference was over. I hurt him, too. Just like his ex fiancée did."

Maddie sighed. "So what's next?"

Kennedy gazed at them both through watery eyes. "I

guess we just sit back and ring in the New Year."

. . .

Matt poured a small sampling of recently bottled cabernet and swirled his glass to open the wine up a bit. After breathing in deep to catch the dark cherry and coffee notes of the wine, he tasted it.

Good. But not great.

Although truth be told, since he'd last seen Kennedy over two weeks ago, he hadn't tasted a single wine that bordered great. Maybe it was him. He was losing the sensitivity of his taste buds. Or he just plain couldn't concentrate. He looked down at the wine journal Kennedy had gotten him for Christmas and snapped it closed. How the hell could he concentrate on anything when he had that reminder of her in front of his face?

He thought of her often. Even read a favorable write-up about her company in the newspaper last week, despite the unique press conference she had given. It seemed as if her honesty about the software she'd created had only enhanced her reputation in the city. That was probably keeping her busy.

And here he was, a man who could barely remember to brush his hair let alone taste any of his wines. Some businessman he was.

"Matt," his mom called from the top of the stairs, "are you down there?"

He glanced up. "Yeah, just doing some sampling." *If you could call it that.*

His mom carefully made her way down to the cellar. "Justin is looking for you," she said mildly.

"He's here?"

"Yes, catching up with Jim right now. He got a promotion at work, so he's taking a few days of earned time off."

"I'm happy for him. At least he got one thing he wanted."

She eased herself into the chair next to him. "Pour me a taste, please," she said.

He did as he was asked and slid the wine glass toward her. She swirled the contents a few times then held the glass up to her nose just as he'd done. "Wow, this is delicious, dear," she said with an enthusiastic smile. "Dad would be so proud. Your best to date."

He frowned at the bottle. "Is it?"

His mom sighed as she set her glass down on the table. "Matthew, you have been in a complete funk since New Year's. I told you that I'd always have an ear for anything you wanted to talk about. So tell me what's going on with you."

"Nothing's going on with me. Shouldn't you really be asking Justin this? He was the one who just broke off his engagement."

"Yes, and I have spoken to him. He seems to be handling the breakup with Kennedy better than you have. Better than any of us, actually."

"Yeah, well, I told you from the beginning she didn't belong with him."

"Who *does* she belong with, then?"

He looked up and met her knowing gaze. "Did Justin tell you?"

She shook her head. "He didn't have to. Honey, I'm your mother. Plus, I hate to tell you but you don't have the poker face you may think you have. In fact, you look awful. Like a man who's had a woman on his mind these past few weeks."

He brushed a hand through his hair and blew out a deep breath. "Yeah, I'm sorry, Mom."

She chuckled. "Sorry for what?"

"Hell, I don't know. For letting you and Justin down."

"Language," she said gently. "People can't control their feelings, just their actions. And as far as I know, you didn't *do* anything. You're a good son and a good brother. You've always taken us into consideration before yourself, like giving up your dreams when Dad passed, staying here and looking after me and Caitlyn, and even now with Justin. If anything, we should be apologizing to you."

"What on earth for?"

"For relying on you too much, not allowing you to live the way you want. I even saw how Justin depended on you to take care of Kennedy while he was away."

"It's okay. You know I would do anything for you guys. Besides, I love living here and running the winery."

She regarded him with a sympathetic half smile. "I know you do. Now. But I also know that most of the decisions you've made in life have been centered around what others have wanted. What do *you* want, Matthew?"

Matt remembered Kennedy asking him that very question not too long ago. He knew the answer then, but could never voice it. Because he wanted something—someone—who belonged to someone else.

"I don't want anything, Mom. Everything worked out for the best. Even for Kennedy."

She gazed into his eyes, a sadness lingering in their blue depths. "Did it work out for the best?"

He was saved from answering when he saw his brother come down the stairs.

"Hey," Justin said, tipping his chin up as he approached.

"Hey." Matt stood, extended his hand to his brother, feeling more than a dizzying amount of relief when Justin shook it. He hadn't spoken to his brother since Justin had punched him in the jaw and was afraid he still hadn't forgiven him.

His mom cleared her throat. "Well, I should let you two talk. I need to go check in on that new girl in the tasting room. I think she's been eating more of the cheese and crackers than the customers." She kissed both her sons, then with one last concerned glance toward Matt, she went upstairs.

Justin pointed at the wine. "I could use a glass of whatever that is."

Matt obliged and poured him a glass. "It's a cabernet."

Justin sat down, stared at the glass without touching it for a few moments. "How's your jaw?" he asked.

"Healed." The one part of him that he could say was. "So I hear congratulations are in order."

One corner of his mouth twisted upward. "Thanks. I lost the girl but got the promotion, didn't I?" He took a healthy mouthful of wine then swallowed. "Hell, Matt, you were right. I do have screwed-up priorities, which is why I'm home visiting. I'm trying to become a little less me centered. Mom's so happy. In fact, if you need any help with the winery while I'm here…"

Matt sat back, shaking his head. "We're good. You enjoy your vacation."

Justin fingered the stem of his wine glass for a few seconds, looking thoughtful. "So, have you talked to Kennedy?" he finally asked.

Matt laughed. "No. Why would I?"

"You told me you liked her."

"Yeah, well, I like Dustin Pedroia and the Red Sox, but you don't see me trying to contact them."

"You would if you could," he said, his lips curving into a slight smile. "Besides, this is different and you know it. You cared for Kennedy enough to travel all the way into Boston that day of her press conference. That says something, that you like her a lot. I mean, I was engaged to her and couldn't travel ten minutes to be there for her."

Matt shrugged. "All right, I like her a lot, okay? More than I've liked a woman in a long time. And I haven't even the foggiest idea why. She's ridiculously anal, has a chocolate addiction that rivals mine, owns more eyeglasses than some people have underwear, and has enough anxiety to fill a psychiatric ward two times over."

"Yeah," Justin said wistfully. "I liked those things about her, too."

"She also has a heart for people and for bringing them happiness."

"You should go to her and tell her that, then. Hell, I never did."

Matt blinked, caught off guard by his brother's suggestion. Was he really saying what he thought he was saying? "No, it wouldn't be right. I would never do that to you."

Justin leaned over and clasped him on the shoulder. "Look, I'm not exactly giving you my blessing here, but I have had some time to think and to talk to Mom. You've made enough sacrifices for our family. Maybe this time, you should do what you really want to do. Because as I see it, you forgot to mention that Kennedy is also smart. Smart enough to recognize when she was making a mistake with me before it was too late."

Matt sat there and listened to his brother's words with a mixture of elation, hope, and guilt. He wasn't even sure if Kennedy would have him, but he had to try and not hold back his feelings. It was about time he did do something for himself—what *he* wanted to do and not because he had to do it.

Matt's thoughts began to shoot off in his head like fireworks, causing his legs to stall, keeping him planted where he was.

"You should go to her," his brother urged. "It wouldn't have worked out for me. But maybe, maybe it could work out for you."

• • •

A knock on her office door had Kennedy snapping herself at attention. Her mind had been a thousand other places—namely on Matt and the rest of the Ellis family. She missed them so much. She should be concentrating on selecting one of the new ad campaigns the PR firm had come up with, but her heart just wasn't into it. She'd made a mess of her love life. How could she possibly think about helping others with theirs?

"Come in," she finally called.

Mia walked in with a coffee, closing the door behind her. "How's my favorite boss doing today?" she said, setting the mug down on her desk.

Kennedy rolled her eyes. "I would dial down the kiss-ass, if I were you. I doubt we'll have the money for bonuses for quite some time yet."

Mia chuckled. "Well, I have a feeling it won't be as long as you think. From my perspective, business is up and morale is good. In fact, that's why I'm here. You have some clients waiting to see you now."

"Clients?" Kennedy glanced at her schedule and frowned. "I don't have any appointments today."

Mia shrugged. "I didn't see it on your schedule, either, but the hot guy and his family were quite insistent that they needed to see you today."

"Well, you're just going to have to—"

Hot guy…

And his *family*? Pulse thumping, Kennedy jumped out of her chair and scurried to the door.

Matt was there in the reception area.

Her heart burst at the sight of him. He was tall and handsome with that hint of a beard he had growing in. All the air seemed to leave her lungs at that moment, and she had a hard time making her tongue work.

"Matt," she whispered, walking up to him. "What are

you doing here?" Then her gaze traveled over his shoulder, and her eyes widened. His mom and Caitlyn stood beaming behind him. "I mean, what are you *all* doing here?"

Matt shrugged. "They insisted on coming along."

Caitlyn elbowed her brother. "Hey, I hardly ever get to Boston. Mom even let me skip school."

"Well, it is a special occasion and all," Barbara said with a wink.

Special occasion? Kennedy blinked. "It is?"

Matt cleared his throat. "Uh, can we go in your office and talk?" He cast a sidelong glance to his family then lowered his voice. "Just the two of us."

"Oh. Of course," she said, leading him into her office.

Once inside, Matt closed the door behind him and locked it. When she questioned him with a look, he shrugged. "You don't understand. Those two are relentless. I doubt they'll give me two minutes to say what I've come here to say to you before they try to barge in and do it for me. My mom even brought you a fruitcake, for Pete's sake!"

She chuckled, despite the frustration on Matt's face. Oh, how she missed his family. And more importantly, she missed *him*. It was complete bliss to see him again. "What did you come here to say?"

"Two things. First, I wanted to apologize for comparing you to Samantha. You're nothing like her. You're warm and caring and honest—a completely beautiful person on the inside and the outside. You wouldn't put your career ahead of people. I knew all that deep down, I really did, even before you confessed everything at the press conference."

She gave him a watery smile. "Really?"

"Really. But I had to make sure Justin was okay."

"I know. You're a good brother." One of the things she loved about him. "What is the second thing you wanted to say?" she asked, cocking her head.

Matt raked his hands through his hair. "That I'm a mess without you. I'm a complete mess, and despite you just breaking off your engagement with Justin, I was kind of hoping to hear that you were a mess without me, too."

He's a mess without me! Her heart sang with delight, stunning her into silence for a few beats. "Yes! I'm a mess, too."

"Thank God," he breathed. He fiercely pulled her to him, burying his face in the side of her neck.

Tears slipped over her lashes. "I'm not used to feeling this way. But there it is. For so long, I've tried to create this perfect life and the perfect love for myself, but you know what? I can't. I'm just so sorry that I hurt Justin in the process."

He pulled back to look at her. "I think he'll be okay. We had a long talk."

She raised her hands, cradling his face in her palms. "I'm sorry for hurting you, too. It's kind of funny. For a woman who doesn't like messes, I sure know how to create them, don't I?"

His mouth twitched with amusement. "Mmhmm, it's one of the things I find most fascinating about you."

"You do?"

He nodded slowly, leaning his face close to hers. "I do." He kissed her then, long and deep as his arms came up and wrapped around her like they'd never let go.

Kennedy kissed him back, straining into him, her body trying so desperately to melt into his. She kissed him and kissed him until she had to come up for air.

She broke contact, tilting her face back. "That's good," she said, her chest heaving, "because I kind of had a proposition for you—one that doesn't involve cocktail parties at your winery."

Matt stayed right where he was, his expression warm. "I'm listening."

"Well, how about this? I just thought that if you wanted

to, since we're both so imperfect together that maybe, well, we could make future messes…together?"

He gazed up at the ceiling. "Good grief, I think I've corrupted her."

She laughed. "Well, what do you think?"

He grinned and kissed her again. "I think it's perfect."

Epilogue

Music and laughter filled the tasting room of Ellis Estates Winery. Kennedy smiled to herself as she saw friends and co-workers, as well as clients of Match Made Easy, enjoying the Christmas party she'd convinced Matt to have in honor of her company's third city expansion.

Although truth be told, it didn't take that much convincing.

She and Matt had taken their relationship slow at first, due to the complexity of the family ties, but it was working out great, especially since one of the city expansions of Match Made Easy happened to be Cape Fin Island. She stayed at Matt's place whenever she was in town—which she made sure was frequently.

Matt's mom came up to her, kissing her on the cheek. "Merry Christmas, dear. This is a wonderful party. I love the idea of combining a wine tasting with a chocolate tasting."

Barbara looked radiant in a red sequined top and black flare pants. "Well, that was really a no brainer for us. Matt and

I simply decided to combine our two loves and thought it'd make the evening doubly fun."

Barbara's eyes fluttered as she took a delicate bite of a dark chocolate salted caramel. "Oh, yes. Very fun," she said, washing it down with a sip of port. "I'm so happy you convinced Justin to come down for the party, too."

Kennedy's gaze wandered over to the Christmas tree, where Justin and Mia looked to be engrossed in conversation. He leaned in and whispered something in her ear. They shared a laugh, their eyes shining.

Hmm…

Kennedy would have never pictured Mia and Justin together, but now…

Well, lately her matchmaking had been a bit less ridged and more open-minded.

"Uh, yeah," Kennedy said, her matchmaking ideas spinning, "I'm glad Justin came down, too. Although to be honest, it was less me and more Matt you have to thank. Justin's really making it a point to take more time away from work and mix in more pleasure."

Barbara nodded approvingly. "It's been so nice seeing you down here more regularly. I'm glad you've been taking more time away from work, too."

She flushed, thinking of all the time she'd spent on the island this past year—particularly at Matt's condo.

"Speaking of work," Kennedy said, glancing around the room, "where's Matt? I would have thought he'd be hawking one of his newest red blends by now."

"Oh, that's right." Barbara slapped her palm on her forehead. "All this wine must have gone to my head. He told me to tell you he's waiting on the balcony deck for you."

"*Outside?* Now? It must be twenty degrees out."

Barbara shrugged. "There's something there. He said it was for your eyes only."

"Well, I better go before he freezes," she said with a laugh then went in search of her coat.

Matt was bundled up in his navy pea coat and gray scarf as he stood against the railing, gazing out into the vineyard. Her pulse quickened at the sight of him. Would she ever not be plagued by a rush of emotions whenever she saw him? It had been well over a year and she had yet to answer yes.

She closed the sliding door behind her, and he turned around. "Thank God," he groaned. "I feel like I've been standing outside for days. Come here and warm me up."

She chuckled and melted into his arms. "Your mom just told me you were out here. What did you want to show me?"

"Well, I've been thinking about us." He pulled back to look at her.

"*Us?* What about us? Everything has been going great, hasn't it?"

He touched her face. "Call me a greedy man, but I think it can be better."

"How so?"

"By this." He reached into his coat pocket and pulled out a diamond engagement ring. "I love you, Kennedy Pepperdine."

"Oh, Matt," she whispered, her eyes filling up. She'd never seen a more beautiful ring in her entire life, but before she could even begin to tell him that, he took hold of her shoulders and gently positioned her in front of him so she could see out into the vineyard.

"Okay, Jim, hit it!" he yelled down.

Before she could blink, the vineyard lit up with colored lights, making it look like a theme park from Disney World. "Oh my gosh, is this all for me?" she said in awe.

"Look down there," he pointed.

There on the flat land were white lights strung out in words. It read: *Will You Ma Me?* She blinked at them.

He wrapped his arms around her middle and began nuzzling her neck. "What do you say, Kennedy?"

"I'm not sure."

"What do you mean you're not sure?" He looked down for himself then his lips puckered with annoyance. "Oh, hell. It's supposed to say *Will You Marry Me?* Those stupid cheap lights Caitlyn bought. I knew they wouldn't last. I wanted this night to be perfect for us."

She laughed, cradling his grouchy face in her hands. "I love your proposal exactly the way it is. It's so right, because it is so *us*. And that's what makes it perfect to me. And by the way, the answer is most definitely yes. I love you, too," she said against his lips. "I love you so very much."

"Thank God," he groaned, and then pressed his lips against hers.

Kennedy couldn't help but feel a soaring rightness that went on as they kissed and kissed and drank each other in. She loved him and he loved her. Some days were great and some days weren't, but she wouldn't trade any of them for anything else in the world.

"I think I've loved you ever since we got stuck in that elevator, and you pulled out that brown paper bag of yours," he murmured, leaning his forehead against hers.

"Matt Ellis, I didn't know you were such a romantic," she teased. "You used to be so cynical about love."

He grinned. "A certain redheaded matchmaker changed my mind."

"Let's go in and tell your mom and the others about our engagement."

"Not yet," he said, taking her hand. "I want you to myself for just a little while longer."

"Matt, have you lost your mind?" Chuckling, she blew out her breath in the chilled night air for effect. "It's freezing out here."

He pulled her back to him, gathering her into his arms. "I'll just have to work a little harder to warm you up then," he said, burying his face in the crook of her neck.

And suddenly she didn't feel the least bit cold.

Acknowledgments

I had a complete blast writing this book, but, as with all of my books, it takes a village. Well, probably more like a metropolis.

Thank yous and hugs to my super supportive critique group—The Passionate Critters. The name so fits. Special thanks and praise go to Nina Croft and Cynthia Blackburn who became speed readers when I was approaching deadline. You ladies are amazing! Words can't express how much I appreciate the extra time you gave to me.

Thank you to my favorite editor, Stacy Abrams. You gave me such wonderful suggestions and the very best ideas for new scenes for this book. I am forever grateful, because I completely love how it all turned out.

Thank you also to my Entangled Bliss team: Alycia Tornetta, Debbie Suzuki, and Crystal Havens. I appreciate your professionalism and help. I always know my books are in good hands.

Huge thanks and extra kisses to my husband, who kept two teenagers out of the house, entertained, and fed while I worked on edits this summer. Thanks for being so understanding—and not complaining one bit! That's why there are pieces of you in all my heroes.

Lastly, thank you to all my readers. You make writing all the more special.

About the Author

Jennifer Shirk is the award-winning author of sweet (and sometimes even funny) romances for Montlake Romance and Entangled Publishing. Her novel SUNNY DAYS FOR SAM won the 2013 Golden Quill Published Authors Contest for Best Traditional Romance. Recently, WEDDING DATE FOR HIRE became a finalist in the 2016 NJRW Golden Leaf Contest for best short contemporary romance.

She resides in a beach resort in NJ, so when she's not writing or working on her tan, she's taking care of her most treasured possessions: her husband, daughter, guinea pig (Rocco), and dog (Sox).

Check out her website for News and Links: www. jennifershirk.com

And don't forget to join her newsletter for a chance to win monthly giveaways and free ARCs: eepurl.com/Q6TH1

Find your Bliss with these great releases...

MORE THAN FRIENDS
a *Kendrick Place* novel by Jody Holford

Owen Burnett planned on a quiet, easygoing Christmas, and tells a little white lie to keep it that way. But when his family shows up unexpectedly, he pulls the best friend card to ask Gabby to play his fake girlfriend. Gabby's been hopelessly in love with Owen for what feels like forever, but playing his "fake" girlfriend when the entire boisterous Burnett clan visits is easier said than done. Their chemistry might be obvious, but putting their friendship on the line is a risk she can't take.

SNOWBOUND WITH MR. WRONG
a novel by Barbara White Daille

Worst. Day. Ever. After Lyssa Barnett's sister tricks her into reprising her role at Snowflake Valley's annual children's party, she doesn't think anything can be worse than squeezing into her too-small elf costume. Then tall, dark, and way too handsome Nick Tavlock shows up to play Santa...and an unexpected storm leaves them snowbound in the isolated lodge. Now Lyssa is trapped with the man who drives her crazy in more than one way. She needs to stay strong--and far way from the mistletoe. Or maybe she just needs a little Christmas spirit...

CHRISTMAS WITH THE SHERIFF
a novel by Victoria James

After fleeing her beloved small town five years ago, Julia Bailey is back to spend Christmas with her family. Returning is hard, but keeping the devastating secret about her late husband is even harder. Her place isn't in Big Sky Country any longer...but the more time she spends with the irresistible Sheriff who saved her once before, and his adorable little daughter, the more Julia starts wishing she could let go of the past and start a new life.

WHITE-HOT HOLIDAY
a *Real Men* novella by Coleen Kwan

When a volcano grounds all flights back to the States, Aaron Cade finds himself stranded in Oz. For Aaron, family holidays are to be endured, not celebrated. Only Naomi Spencer brings magic to the simplest things: shopping for gifts, finding the perfect decorations, and making him feel at home in the bizarrely tropical December heat. His sudden, overwhelming attraction to Naomi will turn his idea of home upside-down...but can he change everything for one white-hot love?

CPSIA information can be obtained
at www.ICGtesting.com
Printed in the USA
LVOW11s1629110417
530416LV00001B/43/P